ELOQUENT TATTOO

DR. AUDREY LAVIN

ANAPHORA LITERARY PRESS

COCHRAN, GEORGIA

ANAPHORA LITERARY PRESS
163 Lucas Rd., Apt. I-2
Cochran, GA 31014
www.anaphoraliterary.wordpress.com

Book design by Anna Faktorovich, Ph.D.

Cover Design and Illustration: Li Hertzi
Photo of Author: Lauren Shay Lavin

Published in 2011 by Anaphora Literary Press

Eloquent Tattoo
Audrey Lavin—1st edition.

ISBN-13: 978-1-937536-12-1
ISBN-10: 1937536122

Library of Congress Control Number: 2011945566

ELOQUENT TATTOO

AUDREY LAVIN

Important People around Midfield Campus College in Midfield, Ohio:

Abby McKenzie........................Mary Beth's friend and
      college M.D.
Austin Westlake.......................Murder victim
Celeste, Eleanor, Liz, and Robby…...Students at McCollege
Mary Beth Goldberg..................English professor and
      detective
Ted Ruppy.............................Chemistry Professor
Tony Bartlett and Gabe James……..Mary Beth's two boyfriends
      (tut tut!)
Seth, just call me Seth, Yoder.........Sheriff
Sylvester Morse........................His Deputy
Simone Westlake……...Residing in Akron

DEDICATION

Eloquent Tattoo would have never found its way to readers' hands without the support, including good natured criticism, by my husband Carl and the rest of my large family. Thanks to all of you Lavins and Lavins by choice (except baby M. who hasn't put in his two cents—yet) for your help with controlling my blog and the use of your names, from sensible suggestions to punchy puns, and from your photography to needed hand-holding.

I dedicate this novel with love to my family, its good times and values.

ACKNOWLEDGEMENTS

"Silent gratitude isn't much use to anyone." —G.B. Stern

So here's my very public and equally deep appreciation to all of you who have helped Mary Beth and Tony solve the third murder they have stumbled across in their otherwise ordinary careers. I have already expressed gratitude to my supportive family in the dedication. Many others, individuals and groups, have contributed to the strengths of this novel. Some of them are:

The Wednesday Writers Workshop, the Akron Manuscript Club, and the Walsh Writers with additional specific thanks due to Ernie Campbell (computer), Bonnie Demopoluous (surveillance), Charita Goshay (name), Reg Keeland (title critique), Sanfred Koltun (dunes), Mike Ludwig (bicycles), Alan Rinzler (edit), G. L. Rockey (publisher), Alistair Sinclair (Scotch whiskey), and Marge W. (character).

The errors are all mine, but remember, Dear Reader, this is a work of fiction.

PROLOGUE

"Why, I can smile, and murder while I smile,
And cry, 'Content,' to that which grieves my heart,
And wet my cheeks with artificial tears,
And frame my face to all occasions."

—Shakespeare, *King Henry the Sixth*

INTRODUCTION

"Friendship," said Christopher Robin, "is a very comforting thing to have."
—A. A. Milne, *Winnie the Pooh*

Momentous occasions don't announce themselves. They are moments often obscured by routine conversations. So early on Wednesday afternoon that 22nd of September, Mary Beth stood with Austin in front of his shop savoring what was left of the autumnal sunshine. Chatting with the inanity of good friends, they discussed the unusual warmth for the end of September. They admired for the third or fourth time the changing color of the dogwoods that Austin had planted in front of his brightly remodeled, two-story brick building. He had painted his street level shop in colors to be noticed, electric blue and "subtle" lavender.

Austin turned toward his window and, pointing proudly to his gallery sign, asked, "Well, Mary Beth, whatdya think?"

His huge smile left no doubt about his own opinion: The addition of his windowed shop to Midfield's Downtown Center bumped the Center's gentrification up a notch.

As far as he was concerned, the sign alone would have done it. The gold newly outlined, mainly lower-case script was spread across the windows of his double storefront, "AUSTIN'S awesome, authentic art & antiques."

In the few seconds it took to come up with a socially acceptable answer, Mary Beth conquered laughter, submerged her professorial need to delete the over-used "awesome," and decided it didn't make one bit of difference what she said. "People will notice it," seemed an indeterminate enough response. "Though I'm not sure if it will attract customers who really want to purchase art."

"Oh, eventually," Austin said. "Meanwhile my 'a-a-a-a-a' gets me listed in the phone book ahead of 'AA Absolutely-Out-Now! Bail Bonds.'"

Again, Mary Beth saw nothing to gain from contradicting a friend. Thinking back, she was glad she had been kind; who could have predicted the change in emotions she would be feeling four or five hours later?

As it happened, she didn't need to say anything about alphabet-izing. At that minute, a coincidental ringing of both of their cell phones formed a different critical commentary to Austin's remark: Does anyone today use phone books?

Examining the caller I.D. showing on her bright red Samsung ($6.00 extra for the color, but easy to find in her briefcase) Mary Beth's answer to her caller was, "I can call back later."

Austin's colluding smile translated to, "I'll do the same." As he spoke, he emphasized his words by turning off his phone.

In retrospect, Mary Beth felt sick that she hadn't taken the time to finish her conversation with Austin. It wasn't due to any impa-tience on her part. She had planned to talk longer, but in addition to having seen Tony's number on her cell, she also noticed the hour. "Thanks for lunch, Austin, and for showing me your new sign. I have to run. Campus calls me to my 1:30 class."

"Listen, Mary Beth, while we were having lunch, I came to an important decision. No, two. I want you to have this extra key to my shop. You're my best friend in Midfield. Someone should have a key for when I'm out of town or just in case something happens. I'll register you with the alarm service."

Mary Beth felt touched later that night, when she thought more about this overt sign of trust.

Austin continued, "The second thing is big. I'd like to talk to you about it tonight. In fact, I want to lay out the whole megillah. It's got nothing to do with modernism or any ism. It has to do with me. C'mon over and I'll order a pizza."

Austin did not want her to leave. He put his hand on her shoul-der and turned her toward him, "If you don't mind, this will be between just you and me. Anyone else will think I'm a fool. Maybe you will, too. At least tonight you won't be bringing Tony along. He's got that bike club meeting and if that's out early, he'll be hap-py to stay at home and work on that book of his."

Mary Beth remembered that Austin had not merely rested his hand on her shoulder. He tightened his hold until he was almost clinging to her. "Even I'm beginning to think I'm paranoid—or maybe nuts… If, for some reason, I'm not around to tell you ev-erything (see, I said I was paranoid), I've made a tape. You'll know what to do." Austin gave a big grin as he added, "As always. The tape is in my antique cash register under the checks-that-have-bounced pile. Now, you have the key?"

Her answering smile was meant to be reassuring. "OK, you're right. I won't bring Tony, but I will bring a bottle of wine." Realizing now that these had been almost her last words to Austin, Mary Beth burst into tears.

She liked Austin for himself and because, in different ways, they were each other's "the other." Mary Beth's move to Midfield perceptibly changed the percentage of Jews in the small town as Austin's move changed the percentage of heterosexual men outside of the College who were interested in the arts. Midfield was Midwest's football country.

Austin ended the conversation with a few cryptic remarks. "Actually, I planned it that way, just the two of us," he had said with a grin. "I'm a member of the Bike & Hike Club, too, remember? I know when the regular irregulars meet.

"And Tony's fixing the brakes on both of our bicycles, just to make sure. He's the only one among those mechanics I'd let touch my bike after that so-called accident." Austin's grin disappeared as he pulled another phrase from the stock of trite sayings he used to cover deeper emotions, "Houston, we have a problem. I'm not sure if I dare to go on the weekend trip or not; so it won't hurt if I skip the club's planning meeting. See you at 6 p.m."

What does he mean, "dare to go on the weekend trip"? It's probably not important. If it is, he can tell me tonight, she had wondered, but simply said, "See you at 6, Austin." Though a college town with some sophistication, Midfield, Ohio, was in the mid-west: lunch at noon, dinner at 6 p.m.

Hefting her over-flowing briefcase to her left hip, Mary Beth waved goodbye with her free hand. Now, remembering that final, flip goodbye, she hid her face in her hand as she smothered more tears.

CHAPTER 1: LATER WEDNESDAY AFTERNOON

"All farewells should be sudden."
—Lord Byron, 1821

Professor Mary Beth Goldberg's after-class walk later on Wednesday took her from her office in Loomis Hall to Avenue Wine, not that the liquor shop was situated on anything like an avenue. It was on Campus Lane, a two-block street that housed Campus Lane Book Store, Campus Lane Cleaners, and Campus Lane Pharmacy. Someone had to break that rhythm (or monotony), and Leo DiCarlo, proprietor of Avenue Wine, did. The short Campus Lane and Midfield's not-much-larger Downtown Center proudly shared bragging rights as the last hold-outs of the malling of the Midwest. They were the charming parts of town that Midfield Campus College tour guides showed prospective students, especially if they were accompanied by parents.

Mary Beth's brisk walk ended with the purchase of two bottles of New Zealand Shiraz, *one for Austin, one for me. A good way to celebrate the first day of autumn*, Mary Beth figured. The short burst of exercise had energized her for any unforeseen complexities to be found in Austin's mysterious dinner, though she had asked herself, *What could be mysterious about sharing a 6 o'clock pizza with a friend?* She arrived exactly on the hour, proffered wine bottle in hand, and climbed the stairs to Austin's apartment over his shop. It had been decorated by one of his trendy ex-girlfriends, but it wasn't trendy this evening.

Entering the hall and living room through the partially opened door made her feel somewhat edgy, almost disgruntled, most certainly not her usual gruntled self. She realized her feelings of unease were caused by Austin's disorienting configuration of furniture. "This from a man who even arranges his shoes by *feng shui*?" she asked the rather fetid air.

Antique dealer, collector, and good friend Austin Westlake had been educating Mary Beth about mid-century modern designers for the course in mid-century modern novelists she planned to teach at Midfield College Campus next semester.

Mary Beth was determined to show influences back and forth. So far the only similarities she could find were in the furniture designers' and 1950s writers' reaction against the past. "Both groups of creative people were seriously into experimentation," she wrote in her notes for a future lecture. Unable to draw any more original conclusions, she mentally shrugged her shoulder and made a promise to herself to check with Austin again.

Now recalling those thoughts of experiments and radical points of view, she tried to re-orient herself to the room. Austin's serious collection of furniture had been lined up with two Eames chairs, a leather footstool, and Paul McCobb bench leaning against walls to barricade the windows facing the street and blocking the door to the steps leading up from his shop. The heaviest piece of furniture in the room, an original Robsjohan Gibbings Mesa table, looked as if it had recently been pulled away from the door to allow her to enter. She noticed the Widdicomb table with its drawers erratically opened. *What's this all about? Austin, where is he?*

She called his name as she looked first in his bedroom, then the office. There he was in all the sartorial splendor of his blue velvet jacket with sleeves pushed up in an affected casualness that allowed Mary Beth to see a tattoo she hadn't noticed before.

I wonder if there are more, Mary Beth inwardly smiled at where her thoughts were leading her.

Austin's head was resting on one arm on his desk, so Mary Beth called out again, "Come on, Sleepy, your company is here."

Walking over to the Eames desk chair and trying to shake Austin awake, Mary Beth was more aware than she had been of his heaviness and got a closer look at the new tattoo. *What is that all about? A lop-sided circle, a mystic society? I've sure never seen that before.*

And that smell? Ugh. Even his Armani spray cologne couldn't disguise it. The fetid smell she had noticed on entering the apartment was worse the closer she moved to Austin.

Other visible evidence of soiled trousers, blue lips, and dilated eyes suddenly coalesced. Mary Beth yanked her hand from his stiffened shoulder. She realized that Austin wasn't going to wake up—ever.

He had been fine a couple of hours earlier, she thought, more than fine. At lunch he bragged about the results of his physical at the Cleveland

Clinic and was close to obnoxiously expansive about his new storefront.
Something is decidedly wrong here.

She forced herself to carefully put the bottle of wine down on the desk. She carefully put herself down on a chair. She bent her head between her legs to keep from passing out. Then she called 9-1-1. As soon as she finished the emergency call, she speed dialed Tony's cell. He would know what to do. He always did. He had fixed her bike, talked her through tenure problems, and helped her solve two murders that had previously and inexplicably crossed her path.

The line was busy.

Advantages of small town living became almost immediately apparent. In response to her 9-1-1 call, the city of Midfield's three teams that would take charge arrived. They came just a few minutes after the failed call to Tony. They didn't have to travel far.

First on the scene was Midfield's single Basic Life Support ambulance crewed by the three-member EMT team. They pulled on white cotton gloves as they entered the apartment. While their volunteer took notes, the two professionals, the paramedic and his CPR certified driver, finding no respiratory or cardiac activity, made an immediate determination of death. They ignored Sheriff Seth's new assistant, Sylvester, who swaggered behind them into the room.

Seconds later, Mary Beth felt everything was under control when her friends Abby McKenzie, the doctor affiliated with both the college and police department, and Seth Yoder, Midfield's only detective, only sheriff, and newly elected chief of police arrived. They, too, pulled on the required gloves as they entered a potential crime scene.

Running across the room, Mary Beth almost threw herself at Seth, who defended himself against the onrush of her slight frame with a quick twist of her wrist. She still managed to push him closer to the inert body than he liked, as she half-sobbed, "Sheriff Seth, I've never been so glad to see anyone in my life."

"Just call me Seth, Mary Beth."

"Oh, I thought while you were on duty I should be more formal."

"Just call me Seth and calm down a notch or two or you'll be making the best speech you never wanted to.

"Now tell me, Mary Beth, are you OK? And what are you doing

here?" Mary Beth shuddered as she pointed to Austin's seemingly resting form. She speed-dialed Tony again in the minute it took for Seth to walk over to the body, causing the paramedics to step aside. He immediately took in the situation. Seth wouldn't be the one to accelerate literary analysis of a novel, but he was a quick read when it came to a corpse.

"I want to ask you a few questions now while everything is fresh."

Mary Beth grimaced at the term "fresh" being applied to Austin's body. Worried that she was going to throw up, she dug her nails into her palms to gain control. While she had it, she quickly answered Seth's questions about her discovery and why she was at Austin's in the first place.

"It looks as if someone has been kicking the desk recently. It wasn't me, I. The wine bottle is from me. I, no, me. I'm sorry about it, Seth. I didn't mean to disturb the scene of the crime."

"I know. I know. Now tell me about seeing Austin earlier."

"Well, first I should tell you, or maybe not." She continued in a hurry when she saw the impatient expression on Seth's face. "I think Austin has a new tattoo. Anyway I don't remember seeing it before. Of course, I don't remember the last time I saw him in a short-sleeved shirt. It must have been last August. Do you think he joined a secret society?"

"You've been reading too much Dan Brown. I'll look into it. Doesn't look like anything very much from here. Maybe his girlfriend is named Ophelia or he's crazy about that Ophrah show. Now what did he have to say earlier today?"

"When I saw him this afternoon, he wasn't his usual sanguine-self. He mentioned he had something to tell me," she said, "but now I'll never know." *Or will I?* she wondered as a sudden memory penetrated.

"I might be here for a while, Mary Beth. Sometimes it takes a longer time to circle the wagons than you might think. I'll get back to you later. I know you're not running away." He turned from Mary Beth for the minute. Medical and technical details took immediate precedence.

Dr. Abby McKenzie was giving her preliminary report to the Sheriff's Department; that is, to Seth. Her formal forensic science approach included all available information on approximate time of death and how she arrived at it. Seth knew the process well; he wanted to hear results. "If we assume that 98° is normal and the body is cooling at the rate of 1½ degrees per hour and we see," Abby said with an emphatic wave of the thermometer "we see a present temperature of 94°; we can pretty well figure that death occurred about 2 1/2 hours ago. I'll give a more definitive report after I've examined stomach contents.

"Right now, all I can say is that it's death, and not by natural means. I've ruled out stroke, heart attack, and a dozen other natural reasons. That means we're looking at a probably homicide, by undetermined means."

"Thanks, Abby. More later? In my office, right?"

"Yes, Seth, after the autopsy when it's all cut and dried. I like the sense of closure," she said with a straight face.

Seth turned, almost permitting a smile. "I don't want to debase this S.O.C. That means no more rushing me, Mary Beth. Physically and other ways speed can be the enemy of a police investigation. We follow forensic protocol here."

He addressed Abby again, "I've gotta trace the outline of Austin's body before you and your EMT boys haul it away to your lab." As the lab was located on the ground floor of the police department to facilitate entrance and exit of dead weights, it would be easy for Seth to check the corpse again post-autopsy. But preliminary work had to be done immediately. Seth concentrated. Tracing a sitting body was at best an awkward job.

Sylvester was making it more awkward. It didn't take any special ability to interpret Seth's angry looks directed at him. He pulled on his cop shades and hid behind them while he apologized, "Sheriff, I'll be finished dusting for fingerprints in a minute. I'm just covering this part of the room: the desk, desk chair, bottle and other stuff on the desk, maybe a few other things."

Mary Beth was carrying on another conversation—with herself. "I have to keep calm. I have to." she said speaking audibly as she stumbled to the farthest Eames chair and speed dialed Tony again. This time she left a message. She watched, as if from another dimension, while Austin, or what had been Austin, was made ready to go to the M.E's office for forensic examination. His body was placed in a black plastic body bag.

Plastic, she thought. He'd die! He was so seriously anachronistic.

_Even the helmet he wore on that last bike trip was an old leather "beater,"
a genuine padded "hairnet."_

Abby interrupted Mary Beth's thoughts by giving her an affectionate pat on the back, saying, "I'm finished now. Sorry to say, so is your friend. Call you later." Mary Beth understood the touch if not the words, because by then, she was listening to Seth's request.

"Mary Beth, please sit on the other side of the room. Do not touch anything, including your wine bottle. I don't want the scene any more contaminated than it already is. We're gonna put up crime scene tape now." Mary Beth nodded assent even though Seth couldn't see her and even though she sat rooted, mesmerized by the unreality of the situation.

Tape? What did Austin say about a tape he'd made? Something he wanted me to listen to? That memory penetrated again. _A tape was downstairs in the shop. In the cash register? What had he said? Why didn't I listen? I've got to remember. It was only a few hours ago._

CHAPTER 2: MORE ON WEDNESDAY

"Lit happens."
  —Popular Saying, 20th Century

After lunch with Austin, Mary Beth had hurried back to campus, arriving a few minutes late for her "American Romantics" class, a study of Whitman, Dickinson, and Poe. She made the deadline with more than five minutes to spare before the unwritten campus rule kicked in. Un-codified in student handbooks, it was one of the few laws that 100% of students adhered to: "If prof is fifteen minutes late, students don't have to wait."

"We almost caught you, Mary Best," Robby Sayers had called out from the first row.

"Mary Beth," was the not so stern correction. The college's insistence on a democratic culture led students to address all faculty members by first names, but Robby's use of a pet name he'd overheard Tony Bartlett use crossed an invisible line into inappropriate familiarity. Because she was a friend of his family, Mary Beth fought a losing battle with Robby trying to subtly remind him that the woman who was a family friend and frequent guest in his house had to be regarded in a different light from the same woman who was his lit professor. *At least I know Robby by name, she thought. Inwardly smiling, she added, and by the ostentatious gold ear-stud he sports.*

This year memorizing student names was more difficult than last; the fads of changing appearances every day by experimenting with piercings, coloring, or tattoos had arrived in the heartlands.

Mary Beth liked this infusion of individuality and could laugh at the added confusion it brought to her class. She was enjoying her second year as a visiting professor. She suppressed a blush as she admitted to herself that her new and secret e-boyfriend added to the excitement.

After class, Mary Beth had headed back to her Loomis Hall office, preoccupied with a typical self-made, non-problem of student identification.

Then a compromise, *Just a quick check of e-mail.* One look and that promise she had made to herself turned immediately into disappointment and a long scolding. *Don't be so ridiculous, Mary Beth. You don't even know the guy. What do you care if he writes or not? You're getting worse than Poe and his romanticized lost loves. A brisk walk is what you need. That and a bottle of wine for Austin.*

Later that Wednesday afternoon, as she was mourning quietly in Austin's apartment, her reminiscences of the afternoon's activities with him and with her class were abruptly interrupted by a typical Sylvester shout, "All civilians out." She looked around. She was the only "civilian" there. Recently appointed, Syl's desperate need to show authority was constantly on display. It was hard for Mary Beth to believe that Midfield had a crime rate that called for another deputy sheriff after the forced resignation of Dwayne Miller.

It was hard for *The Daily Record* to believe it, too, though Sylvester gave the newspaper's editor someone beside the governor to regularly and savagely attack. And attack he did. Syl, designated 'the anti-Seth,' was an easy target. He was never seen without his mirrored sunglasses and jacket opened just wide enough to show one of his collection of huge belt buckles that looked like phony wrestling trophies. In addition, his unfortunate name gave excuse for unflattering Syl-ee and Syl-ph-like puns without giving equal excuse for libel.

Still, that hour of fading into the background of the investigation and waiting for Seth's orders helped. She had remembered the important part of her talk with Austin, where she was to search for the tape.

"I'll leave in a minute," she called over her shoulder as she stood up. Filled with apprehension, Mary Beth pulled the bench back from the door it was blocking and started down the steps. It was getting dark. More time had passed than she realized. She turned on the lights. *Is this trespassing?* As always, she was second guessing her actions. *Am I invading Austin's privacy? I remember now that he asked me to search, but...*

Yes. The tape was in the antique cash register, under a few bounced checks. *I ought to show the checks to Seth. Maybe they mean something. I should show him the tape, too, but I'd better listen first. Maybe it has nothing to do with the crime. Maybe it has something to do with Austin's sex life. I've wondered.* She caught herself, embarrassed that at a time when she should be feeling sad, she had prurient curiosity. She found the tape player on a shelf with other electronic odds and ends and started to listen to a scratchy and somewhat shaky rendition of Austin's voice.

CHAPTER 3: WEDNESDAY

"It is hard to fight an enemy who has outposts in your head."
  —Sally Kempton, *Esquire*, 1970

"Mary Beth, if you're listening to this tape, then it's after the fact" Austin's voice broke. It sounded as if he was crying. The tape continued, "It's after the fact of me." Unfortunately, she already knew that. The remains of the Austin who had made this tape were almost directly above her being stuffed into a body bag.

"I don't have to explain the furniture barricades or that the eeriness isn't all on my side. If you're listening, it means I wasn't paranoid after all. Though this is one time I hate to be right. So much that I was afraid of, I couldn't explain because it depended on the tone of voice or on a quick glance, even on unexpected pauses that gave emphasis to words that were innocent enough in themselves. But kiddo, aren't almost all words innocent until spoken or written?

"It started about two weeks ago. What I'm trying to say is that it happened two weeks before I made this tape. I can't tell when you'll be listening to it. That would mean, Oh, My God, that would mean I could tell when I'm going to die."

Mary Beth turned up the volume and sat down.

"I'm mixed up, Mary Beth. I'm panicky and I'm sure it shows, but I can remember every detail. Well, I can't remember the exact date of my trip. It must be on my calendar. You can check it out.

"It was on one of the last flights Air Tran had scheduled between Chicago's Midway airport and Cleveland's Hopkins. As long as the flight was delayed on the tarmac (Surprise!) at Midway, I was glad I was sitting next to this guy named Nat Amster. It turned out, as those things do, that Nat had gone to Northwestern University when my sister Simone did. Could you believe it, Mary Beth? Of course, Simmy is the beauty in our family, so no surprise that Nat remembered sitting next to her in Dr. Lee's General Semantics class. That made him practically an old friend of the family. Plus, he's a terrific raconteur. His stories invariably featured him as the hero and were all based on the premise that he always kept his word even under the most improbable circumstances, but they were consistently entertaining. I was suckered right in.

"Though after an hour of being entertained by Nat, I was getting edgy about take-off… Wait, Mary Beth, there goes my cell phone? Can you hear it? OK. I turned it off. Where was I?

"Oh, yeah, I was happy when the flight attendant finally stepped forward with an announcement. That happiness didn't last long. 'The flight is cancelled due to mechanical problems,' she said, or something like that. They always say the same thing: 'You will be given a voucher for a hotel room for tonight. Unfortunately all airport hotels are fully booked. You can go into Chicago or wait in the airport. The flight will take off at 9:45 tomorrow morning. Blah. Blah. Blah.' The collective sound of 100 cell phones opening put a helluva exclamation point to whatever she was going on about.

"I didn't care who could hear me cursing; I struggled out of my seat belt, thinking *It'll be sitting up all night in the airport for me.* That part must have been more audible than I thought, too, because Nat turned to me and said, 'We're South of Chicago now. It's just a short drive to my cabin in the Indiana dunes. My car's in the lot. Why don't you just come with me? No one's in the cabin, but I keep it stocked.'

"It didn't take me long to figure out that Nat's hospitality would be a welcome relief from my initial choice, geez, think of it, a night trying to find rest in a crowded, smelly, noisy airport.

"I followed my new buddy off the plane. As we got into Nat's Jaguar, he smiled, 'You'll really like this place.' I was so out of it by then, I couldn't tell if he was making fun of himself or not when he kept saying the same stuff over again, 'Yes, you will. As you know I always keep my word, and it's a great getaway. My parents died in a car accident just after building it and left it to me.'

"We drove for an hour, maybe an hour and a half. I kept dozing and lost track of time. When we came to a stop at the front of the house, I realized that my concept of cabin was a little rougher than Nat's. The 'getaway' was a beautiful log house built as close to the dunes and the shore of Lake Michigan as zoning would permit.

"As Nat unlocked the front door, this golden retriever leaped on us. One really happy pup." Mary Beth could hear the smile in

Austin's voice as he remembered the dog.

"'The Vet's picking him up first thing tomorrow morning,' Nat explained. 'Meanwhile he has the run of the house, don't you, Hector?' he asked as he affectionately rubbed the pup.

"'It's a shame your parents didn't have a chance to live here,' I said, trying to be polite through the daze I was in.

"Nat reflected a minute and said. 'Oh, I think the fun for them was all in the planning. Don't you think they did a fine job, though they underestimated traffic sounds?'

"Nat showed me my room and bath. I felt half asleep, but before going to bed I called Simone to tell her of the coincidences of the evening. You can call her and check on this, Mary Beth. I'm so nervous now, I can't remember her phone number, but she's listed in the Akron phone book.

"'Nat Amster?' she repeated when I told her. 'I don't remember anyone with that name.'

"He says he knows you. From N.U. and General Semantics class.'

"Simone laughed at me or maybe she was laughing at her recollections when she said, 'Oh, that Nat Amster. The weirdo, the pre-Goth Goth. You met him? I thought for sure he'd be locked up someplace by now.'

"'Well, not exactly." I told her I couldn't talk about it now… You know, couldn't talk about it then. You know what I mean, Mary Beth. He was there for Pete's sake. I said something like, 'Talk with you after Akron and car pick up. G'bye, Sis.'

"Smiling at Simmy's remark, I put off sleep another half hour and joined mine host—that's Nat—in the living room. We shared a ham sandwich, not that we needed an excuse to have a post-prandial brandy. 'My cardiovascular surgeon suggested the substitution of a post-prandial walk, but I like this better,' he said.

"I loved those few minutes of peace and quiet that followed, Mary Beth. I could actually hear the lake and only the lake," Austin continued.

Mary Beth was struck by Austin's continued use of her name: *It means that this tape was recorded specifically with me in mind. How eerie. It means that Austin was counting on my solving the problem if anything went wrong. And it sure has.*

While she was thinking, Austin's voice on the tape played on,

"When I explained how I felt to Nat, he said, 'My parents used to say the same thing, but I told you they were wrong. An occasional truck does go by in the distance.' As if to prove his words, the very distant sound of a truck could be heard.

"That's when Hector started to bark, and bark he did as long as the sound lingered in the air.'

"Now listen, Mary Beth. This is important. Nat starts yelling at the dog. Something like, 'Quit that barking, Hector. This isn't the first time I've warned you. If you don't stop that racket, I'll kill you.' Hector's response was to bound over to Nat, and lick his hand.

"To change the subject, I picked up a book by Will Durant from the coffee table and half-heartedly started a conversation on relative merits of Durant vs. Bertrand Russell on the history of philosophy. But we were both too sleepy to keep any conversation going, except the one that ended, 'time for bed.'

"I was out like the proverbial light, waking up just once when something that sounded like a shot or maybe a truck backfiring disturbed my dreams.

"I joined Nat for breakfast. So, you know me. I'm a good guest. I try to make conversation. I ask, 'Is Hector outside already? I miss his smiling face.'

"Then Nat made eye contact and spoke to me very slowly, 'I told him if he didn't stop that damn yapping, I'd kill him.'

"To say I was horror-struck is the worst kind of under-statement. You don't go around shooting your pup because he disobeys you. *What kind of a man is this guy?* I asked myself. *I don't know him.* I realized I had to get out of there. I didn't care how abrupt the change of subject was. I tried to put my thoughts into action. 'Nat, is there any way to get to the airport early. Even here in the Indiana dunes some enterprising person must provide a taxi or shuttle service.'

"Nat laughed. 'It was dark when we drove in. You didn't notice that everyone around here has a three-car garage. There's no business for taxis at all. I'll drive you back and read the paper in the airport. Here, I have an extra one. You take it. Go ahead, take it.' I agreed to Nat's offer, though I never did get around to reading the newspaper he forced on me. What kind of a choice did I have? Believe me I was working hard not to sound or appear in any way judgmental. This guy was too erratic to fool around with. I was determined to keep everything on a pleasant level.

"So I kept quiet while Nat left a note for the cleaning woman and tried to keep the conversation impersonal by telling a few jokes while we stowed our gear in the Jag. As we headed back to Midway Airport, I continued my stand-up routine, 'A high priced lawyer, a low priced lawyer, and a tooth fairy were sitting at Fedeli's bar with a $100 bill between them. The lights went out for a second. When the lights went back on, the $100 had disappeared. Who took it?' In spite of the circumstances I was in, I was laughing in anticipation. I could hardly wait to get the answer out. 'The high priced lawyer of course. The other two are just figments of the imagination.'

"Nat thought that was pretty funny. 'But I've got a better one,' he said. 'If you don't die laughing at this one, I'll have to finish you off.'

"He proceeded to tell a joke, one that I've repeatedly deleted from my e-mail in the two years it's been making the rounds (What happens when someone drops a piano down a mine shaft? A flat miner.) But y'know, I'm a social being, so I gave him something up a grade from a polite smile and made some ha ha, slightly humorous sounds.

"Then it was my turn to tell another joke. I turned toward Nat and started, 'a rabbi a priest and a...' I couldn't go on. Nat's hands were tight on the steering wheel. Honest, his knuckles whitened before my eyes. My slightly humorous response to his joke was less enthusiastic then he had expected. The rest of the trip was in dead silence. I had seen a look in Nat's eyes, that I-always-mean-what-I-say look I had seen at breakfast. Honest to God, I remember it clearly—two weeks later while I'm making this tape for you, Mary Beth. I know I sound peculiar, but this was the look that motivated me to move chairs and tables around the apartment to barricade it.

"Good luck with that Mid-century Lit class, Mary Beth. If you're listening to this tape, I'm afraid it means I won't be able to help you with it anymore."

Austin's voice broke.

The tape clicked off.

This is crazy, Mary Beth thought as her eyes filled with tears again. *It's impossible*. But unconsciously she backed away in horror from the tape player. Consciously, and wondering if she was committing a crime, she grabbed the tape and stuffed it into her jean pocket.

She could hear Seth calling, "Mary Beth, get yourself back up here. That's a potential crime scene down there." She pulled herself together, patted her hair in place, and quickly ran upstairs, guiltily feeling the slight weight and bulge of the tape against her leg. Seth didn't even notice her. He was busy with assistant Syl, who doubled as a crime scene specialist. Syl's assignment was to gather available electronics as potential evidence: computer from the downstairs office, lap-top from the apartment, and cell phone from Austin's desk top.

"I can check out some of these," he said. "You know darn well, Seth, that I don't have the time and we don't have the manpower to do a complete digital dragnet."

Syl didn't bother to turn from his work as he brusquely dismissed Mary Beth, "Don't you dare go near the fingerprint powder, Professor. At this point in time, you can see we're still doing important work here, finishing with the crime scene tape and taking photos."

He stood up, reaching his full height, in order to proclaim, "I'm the one who has the serious electronic responsibilities. I haven't even had time to get downstairs to the main office. What in the…?" He struggled, "What in the heck were you doing there? I hope you didn't touch the computer. You might not understand the difference between shutting it down and pulling the cord. That's what I'm doing now, the right thing to do. This way we can get Computer Forensic Investigators who can retrieve deleted stuff. Us, real detectives, don't need tourists looking over our shoulders. Call Seth's office for an appointment, and stop by in the morning for questioning."

Mary Beth didn't trust Syl and didn't want to disturb Seth. She determined to give the sheriff the tape in the morning.

Back in the security of her home, while nervously eating all of the ice cream in her freezer, Mary Beth googled, "Nat Amster." Nothing worth noting showed on her screen. She took a minute to microwave some dark chocolate to pour over the ice cream. She checked her e-mail. Another downer. Nothing from "Gabe James," the name her secret e-mail friend was using. *I hope it's real, she thought. I hope he's for real. That name sounds fake*, she admitted to herself.

She couldn't reach Tony either as he was spending the day in Akron at a bike sale, then going straight to his bike club meeting. *What do I care? I can get along without a man for physical or emotional relaxation, I think.*

She took her other personal favorite sedative, reading a detective story. This one took place in Africa. It was so enjoyable that she had forgotten that she had originally started it with the hopes it might help her to understand her student Celeste's African background. Tony might have taken her mind off her problems more efficiently, but Mary Beth's other two well tested cures for insomnia (ice cream and murder mysteries) worked as expected. Mary Beth slept surprisingly well and rose early and happy.

CHAPTER FOUR: THURSDAY MORNING

"Always do what you are afraid to do."
—Ralph Waldo Emerson

The morning's optimism was rewarded with an e-mail from Gabe. There it was between JCrew's final, final Final Sale, and "Enlarge Your Penis," waiting in her new-mail box. Keeping up the suspense was part of the adventure of her romance-at-a-distance, a romance that had moved quicker than expected, as e-mail relationships do. She took deliberate time to delete or spam her unwanted mail. Then she opened Gabe's. The message knocked all of the fake romanticism out of her. She could no longer idealize someone she didn't know.

Gabe wanted to come to Midfield.

"I've become addicted to your e-mails, Mary Beth. The way to cure my addiction is to face it head on. I can be in Midfield Monday night. I'm planning to arrive at 6 and leave at 9 pm. Unless, of course, you'd prefer my staying overnight. Think about it. Tell me where to meet you. Don't worry. I will know you. I do know you."

She answered at once, stopping only to think that she did not want to meet him at That Place on Main Street, the restaurant she always thought of as hers and Tony's special place. "Let's meet at Ye Olde Gaol restaurant on the square. I think your leaving at 9 o'clock will be fine, very fine! Remember, Midfield is a small town." She clicked "send." *I hope I don't sound too uptight*, she thought. *I am uptight!*

Mary Beth's uptightness and guilt (*over nothing*, she reminded herself, *nothing—yet.*) increased with a phone call from Tony. "Hi, Mary Best. It was too late to call last night. Wassup?" he added in his best fake street dialect.

"Oh, Tony, I couldn't leave a message. It's too awful. Austin is dead."

"What? A heart attack?"

"No, murder."

"No," his full disbelief was expressed in that one word.

"Yes, they're pretty sure. I'm going to see Seth about it this morning."

"OK. After Seth, can you see me? I know how close you and Austin were. You can be glad now that you were so supportive of him when he broke up with his last girlfriend. Even though she was the last of many," he unnecessarily said, quickly adding damage repair. "I can't help with the murder now. I can give you a hug. You need it and honestly, so do I."

Knowing Tony was there made Mary Beth feel better.

She figured she had time for a brisk walk to cool off before her 8 a.m. class and her dreaded meeting with Seth. The pressure of Austin's tape on her thigh filled her with guilt. She argued with her guilt by reminding herself of the murder on campus she had helped Seth solve. *I'd better get mental instead of emotional juices flowing, the little gray cells working again before I try to face class and Seth.* But the weather that autumn morning was brisker than she was, so she returned home to grade essays before her meetings.

The normalcy of searching for thesis statements worked to get her mind away from Gabe. Student papers over-rode her double worries: what was going to happen Monday night and what had happened not even twenty-four hours ago.

She searched through the jumble of pens that seemed to use her desk drawer for dangerous proliferation activities. For grading and writing comments, she preferred green pens to the more commonly used and to her the more threatening red pens still used by her colleagues. Then she remembered that last night when she was trying almost frantically to relax, she had been reading Alexander McCall Smith who wrote, "There were those who said that writing in green ink was a sign of mental instability."

Am I unstable, Mary Beth asked herself, *Is that why I'm keeping Austin's tape? Couldn't 'stable' be seen as awfully close to the 'rigid' I don't want to be?* In fact, one of her favorite quotes had always been Emily Dickinson's 'A little Madness in the spring/is wholesome even for the King." It felt good to have permission from Dickinson when she wanted to flout the unwritten campus rules on departmental etiquette or "anything else." She squashed that thought of Gabe. But hiding something from the law and from her friend Seth was on a much different level. *I'll take the tape with me.*

Meanwhile, searching for pens and grading a few essays had

brought her precariously close to class time. Thankful for her ability to compartmentalize, Mary Beth gave a mental shrug and went back to her student identification problem. *I have to find a new method to memorize my students' names.* She tried to take advantage of the tendency of people to sit in the same seats at each class meeting, by making a seating location chart as she had in the past. But girl #1 in the first seat, first row, had broken up or had a spat with boy #1, in the second seat in the first row, so moved as far away from him as possible, plus a few students came in late one day. Such trivial incidents resulted in a total re-shuffling of what had seemed like a seating plan.

Next Mary Beth had tried to write two or three key words next to each student's name. "Blond, trendy glasses," she had written next to Liz's registration and, "short, dark curly" next to Celeste's name, bracketing the girls because they came to class and left together during the first week. By the second week, she was stumped. *Who is that girl getting ready for Saturday's football game by dying her hair the school colors? She doesn't look that good in purple and white. And why does she have such bright green eyes?* By the end of class and through the process of elimination, she figured it must be Liz.

Celeste, she had been told, was trying to take two courses that met at the same time. "Why not, if I can do the work night and day?" Celeste asked in her idiosyncratic English as a Second Language. She questioned administrative decisions with the innocent logic of one who had lived her previous life in the non-bureaucratic world of a small community. Celeste was a scholarship student from Lusaka, Zambia. She found that in small-town Ohio, faculty members ignored or stumbled over her last name, Nkolola-Wakumelo. The name signified family and connections where she had grown up–in a village in the Mwinilunga district, remote from the capital. This meant that she was exceedingly fluent in a tribal language that almost no one else, even in Zambia, understood. The little English she had learned at school had been supplemented by the one radio station that reached her village, a station that played U.S. popular songs from the 30s to the 50s.

"Why can't I study American Romantics beneath the moon and under the sun?"

"Because I say so," the Academic Dean replied, and Celeste was forced to drop the class though she was attending twice a week while she negotiated for an independent study credit.

"They can't take that away from me," she insisted to Mary Beth.

Not as tough and persistent as her student Celeste, Mary Beth dropped the key-word method of identification. *Since Robby's the one constant who I know in this class, she figured, maybe I can build a system around how people relate to him. But that's too kooky even for a make-work person like me,* she concluded.

It had been an on-going struggle this semester for Mary Beth not only to identify students in her classes, but also to reconfigure the town/gown relationships of Midfield and the college as they applied to her own social/professional life. At a small bucolic college in a postcard pretty small town, the same people are involved in everything. "We pick each other's' pockets," she'd been informed at the first local fund raiser she had attended.

Her return to campus this fall semester brought with it the feeling of being somewhat in control of her life, if not of all the papers tumbling off her desk. She liked her small office, even her beat-up desk, at Midfield College Campus, better known as M.C.C. or McCollege as students loved to call it. The administration deplored student use of flip nicknames for the college that the P.R. and Recruiting Departments tried to sell as "The Yale of the Midwest." Faculty members laughed at the semantic struggle going on between the two groups.

This would be the year that Mary Beth and her department, headed by Gary Hake, who wasn't her biggest fan, would make the decision as to whether or not she would stay. The search committee had been scrutinizing applicants for a year to find someone to fill the shoes of Dr. W. Stuart Jones, who was now incarcerated and teaching in the state prison. She was one of the three finalists. Was that because she was one of the top applicants or did it have anything to do with her being on campus? As a finalist being called in for a series of interviews, the department wouldn't have to pay for her visit or bother entertaining her. More than once, she had asked herself, *What does the rest of the department really think of my filling the opening I helped create?* As part of that ritual questioning, she was careful to defensively add, *I helped create by the simple act of finding out my predecessor was a murderer.* [See Mary Beth's detective work in *Eloquent Blood*, by Audrey Lavin.]

CHAPTER 5: THURSDAY 22 SEPTEMBER

"All bad poetry is sincere."
—Jay McCarthy

Mary Beth put thoughts of her own career problems on hold along with concerns about Austin's murder and started class with a discussion of the career of the writer who caused the most controversy in her American Romantics class, Edgar Allan Poe.

"Think about Edgar Allan Poe. Think beyond 'The Raven.,'" she said to her class of 22 students, the maximum number permitted by Midfield College, a fact she had to restrain herself from bragging about.

"Never more, never more," came the chant from the back of the room.

Mary Beth acknowledged the quote from the poem and continued her lecture, "Think of that young man when he was your age, scribbling away at poems as many of you do. Only you probably use computers. When you read his poems, remember that he wrote some of them during his teen-age years, when he was misunderstood and as rebellious as some of you might have been."

Robby raised his hand and was called on, "Did he write many letters, too? A friend of mine, you know him ma'am, Austin West-lake, says Poe was an avid letter writer."

Mary Beth struggled a minute with the question of whether or not to stop the class to tell of Austin's death. *Those who know him will hear soon enough*, she decided. *My job is to teach.*

"Yes, Robby, he was," she answered. "Among other subjects he addressed in his letters home was his constant need for money." Her students responded with laughs of identification and agreement, as she knew they would.

Mary Beth continued her lecture, "I'm not saying that you should completely emulate Poe. A guy who died drunk and drugged is maybe not the best role model. But keep in mind that some of his romantic poetry was published when he was your age. It might be a good idea for you aspiring writers to update his vocabulary and compare his poems to yours. And keep in mind that although he later became world famous, he was always misunderstood by the family who raised him."

Later she explained that born in 1809, Poe was orphaned by the time he was two years old. Although John and Frances Allan took him in, they never legally adopted him, and young Edgar had more than the usual adolescent conflicts with Mr. Allan. Everyone in the class could understand that. "To give credit where credit is due," she added, "Though John Allan disapproved of young Edgar's ambition to become a poet, he did pay for his education. But Poe didn't uphold his part of the bargain and gambled. He left the University of Virginia and West Point, which led to a final break with what we would call, his foster family.

"Still, at 18," she reminded the class, "he self-published his epic poem 'Tammerlane.' And who doesn't dream of that?"

The educational methodology of asking her late-teens students to identify with Poe and his poetry worked, or so Mary Beth thought. Her smug appraisal collapsed with the eager waving of two students' hands and the calling out of "Will that be on the exam?" "Will that be on the exam?"

CHAPTER SIX: LATER THURSDAY

"All that we see or seem/is but a dream within a dream."
—Edgar Allan Poe

Seth made it easy for her when she arrived at his office a half-hour after class ended. The door was unlocked, as usual. "The sheriff's office belongs to the people," was Seth's explanation.

He was polite to Mary Beth, at first telling her about the lack of information gained from fingerprinting the scene of the crime. "The only new prints were Austin's and yours on the bottle. We had yours on file from previous times we worked together. Anything else was smeared and old. I'm sending Sylvester back to work the scene some more."

Then Seth began to query Mary Beth and continued to query her over and over again about Austin's death, losing his home-spun friendliness in the process. He was morally above offering to trade information with her, but he did inform her that the so-called tattoo was not a tattoo at all. "It looks like it was something he doodled above his wrist with one of those blue Sharpies on his desk. It's in the rough shape of a circle. Kind of looks like he was drawing a line in it." Seth waited for her response.

None came.

"Now's the time, Mary Beth. Did you see or hear anything you haven't reported?"

Mary Beth's thoughts were back a question. She was still thinking about the non-tattoo. *Could it have been a hieroglyph of some kind?*

Seth moved to the subject that was uppermost in his mind, "Y'know, don't you, Mary Beth, that withholding evidence is a serious crime," Mary Beth gulped and handed over the tape. *How does Seth know everything I'm thinking?*

"Austin told me to search in the old cash register."

Seth pocketed the tape and explained, "He was worried something like this would happen to him."

Remembering the for-your-ears-only message of the tape she had played last night, Mary Beth couldn't believe that Austin had confided in someone else about his fears. "He told you that?"

"Yes, Professor. Austin was anxious about what he perceived as more than one attempt on his life. He mentioned he had left an explanation for you of one of his theories when he came in to discuss another one with me. What else could it be but a tape or a letter? He wasn't into playing games by leaving an obscure clue."

Mary Beth thought of the irregular circle that wasn't a tattoo. *Maybe Austin HAD left an obscure clue. What else could it be? He had drawn a circle and, oh, yes, that wobbly line from the center to the outside rim, the circumference.* Her mind wandered.

She looked up. Seth was still talking. "I don't play games either, Mary Beth, so the information I'm gonna give you isn't in exchange for you giving me the tape. Be thankful that what you're getting in exchange for the tape is not being prosecuted!"

"I know Austin is dead and I'm devastated, but maybe he had good reason for being paranoid. Did he tell you about more than one threat on his life?"

"He was a long way around the barn getting to it, but, yeah, he told me of what he suspected was a planned murder. We have a record of the call back at the station. It was after his bike crack-up a couple of days ago. I should've taken it more seriously. The problem is, and this is why I'm talking to you, the problem is that maybe someone else around here should of been a little more careful."

"What in the world are you talking about Seth?"

"I'm talking about you, Mary Beth."

"Don't be ridiculous."

"Think about it. Were you on the bike trip the day Austin cracked up?"

"It wasn't a real bike trip, just a couple of hours out in the country. Really, a club-ride to the Amish Inn for brunch, and back home. It wasn't even a good brunch, as I remember it."

"Do you remember the bike you were riding?"

"Of course. It was…" Mary Beth stopped. She leaned forward. "On the way to the Amish Inn, I was riding Austin's new Trek. I wanted to try out the seat. That doesn't have anything to do with Austin's death." She could hardly get her correction out, "His murder."

"I have to tell you that when Tony and I go for a long ride, I always end up with a sore butt."

Seth laughed. "I know Tony's interested in your butt, Mary Beth, so was he the one who suggested that you try Austin's bike for the club ride?"

"Sure. Bikes aren't usually gender specific anymore, so it wasn't any problem for me to ride it or for Austin to ride my Cannondale. And Tony said that Austin's saddle with its anatomical cut-out would relieve pressure in the perineum zone." She shrugged her shoulders. "That's the way Tony talks about bikes. I'm always impressed. Austin wouldn't have let me borrow it for a long trip, but for one way to the Amish Inn…oh, my God. You don't think…?"

"Yes. I do, Mary Beth. I have no real evidence, but after the bike trip when Austin told me there had been an *attempt* on his life and again last night when we could all see that there was more than just an attempt on his life, we are faced with the coincidence of y'all being at the same places at the same times. I don't believe in coincidences like your friend Plutarch does."

Mary Beth immediately understood the messages Seth was sending her. The first and surface message was that he didn't believe in coincidences; the second and encoded message was that in his using a quotation from the famous Greek biographer, Plutarch, he was warning Mary Beth, "Seth is smarter than your average cop. Way smarter. He knows more. He reads more. Remember that."

"Seth, I hate to admit it, but I don't know what my 'friend' Plutarch said about coincidences. A little mental refreshment, please."

Seth thumbed a few buttons on his up-graded cell and read aloud, "It is no great wonder if in long process of time, while fortune takes her course hither and thither, numerous coincidences should spontaneously occur."

"I keep a few of these around for dealing with you academic types," he smiled.

He continued to address Mary Beth, "What I know from experience is that a coincidence is a series of events just waiting for an explanation. That's what we've got here. I also know you pretty well, Professor, and I don't believe that you were involved in any nefarious plans to murder Austin. But we can't refuse to look at the strong possibility of you being the intended victim."

Mary Beth had never fainted in her life. Only women in 19th century novels fainted. *I'm not going to start now*, she said to herself as she slipped half-way to the floor. Seth pushed her back in the chair with one hand, handing her a glass of water with the other.

"Don't get so upset. I'm just putting it out there."

During her two years at Midfield College, Mary Beth had learned to put on a faculty-meeting-face at will. Now was the time to put that academically acquired skill into practice and adjust her expression. A good mask. Her "I'm fine" enhanced her fake calm-exterior. It took only a few minutes for that fake calm to be transformed into a genuine calm. The thought of anyone's trying to kill her was too preposterous to take seriously. *I'm just not that important*, Mary Beth objected to herself.

"Where is that bike now?" Seth asked. "I want to see it."

"Which one? Mine or Austin's?"

"It's your Cannondale that was involved in the–we'll-call-it-an-accident-for now."

"Austin said he took it to Bob's Bikes to be repaired. The Trek, the one I was riding, is there, too. Maybe Tony's already fixed them. Does it make any difference, sheriff, if I tell you that Austin's saddle is more comfortable than mine?"

"Mary Beth, I've told you to just call me Seth. And, no, it does not make any difference to me or to poor Austin how your butt felt then or feels now. I think you're still a little dizzy from the shock."

"Can you remember the phone number for Bob's Bikes?" Seth punched in the digits as Mary Beth repeated them, wondering what in the world the bicycle had to do with Austin's post mortem tale of Nat and his presumed threats. *Could the feared Nat Amster have been in Midfield and sabotaged Austin's bike?* She could almost see Seth rolling his eyes at that suggestion.

"Hello. This is Bob at Bob's SuperBikes. We Recycle Cycles."

"Hey, Bob."

"Hey, Seth. Are you taking me up on my suggestion to have bike patrols?"

"No. No sales to Midfield's exemplary police force today. I'm calling about Mary Beth's bike, a Cannondale that Austin brought in for repairs a few days ago."

"Geez, he is a kook. Getting the police after us because we haven't fixed it fast enough for him? We haven't even started working on it yet. Ever since the price of gas went up, our business has doubled. It's great. Even when gas goes down, people have started riding again and like it. Everyone's fixing up old bikes or buying

new ones. If the oil shortage had to be good for someone, I'm glad
it's me. We've even hired an assistant for Tony. I know for a fact
that he hasn't been able to take any time off for months now to
work on his *T. Bartlett's Better Quotations* book."

"Bob, I'm going to interrupt your jabbering. I'm coming by in
a few minutes to examine that Cannondale. It's time to clue you in
on some local problems, too. I want you there at the shop to go over
the bike with me. Maybe Tony, too, but no need to alert him. In fact,
I'd rather you didn't. See ya' in five."

"Mary Beth," he said as he hung up, "any part of this conversation you might have heard is strictly off the record. That includes
off the record to your pal, Tony. I'm letting you ride along the
prairie with me because I know durn well the work you've done in
helping to solve two other murders. The sheriff's department owes
you. But I also know durn well that you are a witness, a possible
victim, and, sorry to say this, we have to consider you as a possible
criminal.

"So, before I go to see Bob, I have a few more questions for you.
I want you to tell me what you remember about the bike trip. Who
was there?"

"I don't know if I can remember, Seth. This is a regular singles
club ride. We all meet the second Sunday of the month in front of
the bike shop. It's open enrollment. It isn't even enrollment. Anyone can join us who wants to. Some of the students always come.
Robby, Liz, and Celeste, who are more or less in my American Romantics class, were on that brunch trip. I remember Celeste's saying, "This trip is hot, too hot not to burn down." But I don't think
she was making a threat. It's just her way of speaking English.

"Townies like Mr. DiCarlo bike with us. Faculty members, too.
Anyone who wants to have a little exercise on Sunday without in-
vesting too much time or energy in it. And there's always the possibility of meeting someone interesting. Last year we had a couple
who met on one of our single rides and got married. That revved
up attendance for a while. Then they got a divorce."

Seth took note of the names for further questioning, and
stopped Mary Beth's flow of unnecessary information. "I have an
appointment now, Mary Beth. Well, you know that," he added. "I'll
have more questions for you later."

CHAPTER 7: STILL THURSDAY

"There is an eloquence in true enthusiasm."
  —Edgar Allan Poe

As Seth later told Mary Beth, he had hurried out of the sheriff and police offices, now housed in the old *Daily News* building, glad again that Midfield had stayed a small town. He liked being part of a community where the old values were preserved. Not only cycles were recycled, but buildings were, too. *Waste not, want not*, he thought.

He nodded to some of his cronies as he passed them taking in what remained of the late afternoon sun. His three buddies were seated on the antique wrought iron bench he had placed in front of his office. He was proud to tell Mary Beth that he had been pleased with himself for buying the bench from Austin and donating it to the police force. It fit right in with the three-storied building's old grey stone exterior. The nineteenth century edifice where the newspaper that preceded *The Daily Record* had been published had needed only a slight modernization to become the new police department.

Not to be outdone in demonstrating the flexibility of law enforcement, the old jail next to it on the square had needed only another slight modernization to become a trendy new white-table-cloth restaurant, Ye Olde Gaol.

Seth said he stopped his mental meanderings with a start. He then turned around and took his time walking back to where his three street-buddies were sitting. "Hey," he said, repeating the conversation for Mary Beth.

"Howdy, Sheriff," Irwin, the only member of the triumvirate not reading *The Record* replied.

"Just call me Seth." was the dutifully uttered next line of the ritual.

Daryl turned to page 3, *Weather*. "Warm enough fer ya'?" he asked.

A pause ensued in the stimulating conversation.

Seth picked up the reins of discourse, trying to guide it. "Seen any people going into Austin's Wednesday afternoon, Irwin?"

"No, I ain't. Jist that there teacher he's friends with or maybe she's larnin' him something."

"Then that bunch a'kids," Joe reminded him. "Must a'been three or four."

His buddies, who were now all listening, nodded in agreement, mumbling something that sounded more like "See ya' later" than anything else.

Seth nodded and continued on his way. He took mental notes of the conversation not only for Mary Beth, but also to add to his Austin crime file later in the day.

Mary Beth had left Seth's office too. Her thoughts were not concentrated on the historic building that presided over the downtown square. As she passed Seth, she only vaguely registered his talking with the men on the bench. Instead, she was worriedly trying to connect the dots between the tape she had listened to and her odd conversation with Seth about her bike. She touched the incriminating tape tucked into her brief case. Of course, she had taken time to make a copy. *Should I have told Seth about the copy?* she asked her better self, the higher Mary Beth. *I'm not withholding actual evidence,* the real Mary Beth answered. *The original tape I gave to Seth is what would be needed for evidence if this ever gets to court.* She wove her rationalization even tighter: *And didn't Austin leave his suspicions for me, Professor Mary Beth Goldberg, not for Sheriff Seth Yoder?*

The murder wasn't simply a puzzle to be solved. Austin had been a close friend. A shudder went through her body when she thought of the scene she had been part of Wednesday night. Her vision was suddenly blurred by tears. She pulled herself together. *I owe Austin. And I can do this.* Her life inside and out of class coalesced. *I'm like Poe's detective Monsieur Dupin at the beginning of "The Purloined Letter." He's contemplating the two crimes he's previously solved in the same way I know that I can help because I've helped solve two murders.* [1] *Like Dupin, I need a plan. First, a conversation with Austin's sister. Then a trip to the Indiana dunes will be in order. Maybe Tony will come with me.*

Typically and unlike M Dupin, she added another layer of unnecessary worries, *What was all this about the bike shop? Seth couldn't*

1   See *Eloquent Blood* and *Eloquent Corpse*.

possibly suspect Tony, could he? Her introspection was of no relevance, and she knew it.

Mary Beth became practical. She wiped the incriminating tear marks from her Oakleys. Tony had bought his-and-hers matching sunglasses for their Hannakah gifts last year, a big step up from Harry the Hannakah Hamster he had given her the year before. "Happy Harry," was Tony's amended name when he put the squeaky running wheel in Harry's cage. "Miserable Mary B." was hers.

Her cell phone rang. *Speak of the devil.* As she said, "Hi," she chastised herself, *I'd better not even think evil if he's going to be under investigation.*

"Mary Babe, can you come on down to the shop now? I know you've finished with classes. You've got a big hug coming, and there's something you have to see."

Tony hung up before Mary Beth had a chance to answer. She continued the conversation, as she often did, with herself. *What the hey, it's only a block. I'll see what's so important now instead of waiting until later.* She changed directions and in a few minutes could see Tony standing in front of Bob's. His 6"2' lanky frame was distinctive, *at least to me,* Mary Beth defended herself against no one in particular, especially unknown no ones who sent her sexy e-mails. His traditional outfit of black jeans and a black t-shirt was equally distinctive on the streets of small town Ohio. Mary Beth took a minute to appreciate his well-constructed "mad scientist" look. Tony worked at being "different." *Perfect. Almost perfect.* When he turned his head to look for her, Mary Beth could see that his pony tail was getting longer and could use a trim. *I'll let him know in a subtle way. Maybe he's emphasizing that his chosen hair style is not a refuge of the balding man.*

They greeted each other with strong, close hugs. Mary Beth liked moving into the security of his strong arms. She noticed that he was, for Tony, well-dressed. "Tony, is this a celebration of some sort? I see you've upgraded your every-day blacks. I like the way your special-occasion Cannonball t-shirt looks on you."

"Look around, Mary Best."

"I am. I've already noticed your best t-shirt. I see you're wearing your Oakleys, too. And you could use a haircut." *Maybe, not so subtle.*

"What else am I supposed to see?" she asked, and quickly answered. "The bike rack in front of the store is full today."

"You're awfully observant about the wrong things. C'mon, Mary Babe, stand back in life. Look at the bigger picture."

She did.

"Tony, is that true?" Mary Beth examined, exulted, and almost exploded at the new sign over Bob's store. Only it wasn't Bob's now. The new sign read, "Tony and Bob's SuperBikes. We recycle cycles and skis."

"Yeah, I thought you'd be excited. It's a combination of things you're interested in, as Whistler says, 'an accident of sentiment and alliteration to the literary man,' or literary woman in this case."

"To-o-ny Bartlett, I thought you were going to give up your *Quotations You'll Use* book. Anyway, that's not what I'm excited about and you know it. In a way, I've felt guilty ever since you followed me to Midfield. That systems research job you gave up might've had a future. No guilt now! You're really co-owner with Bob? How fabulous. How did it happen?"

"Work. Hard work."

Bob stopped his mysterious oiling behind the rack and, remembering to wipe his hands first, came over to shake Mary's hand.

"Sorry about Austin, though I hardly knew him. Life goes on, and congratulations are in order. But you won't be seeing more of Tony, Mary Beth. I told him now that he's half-owner, he'll only have to work half-days. He just has to tell me which twelve hours he wants to work!"

Tony grinned at Bob and his well-worn joke. He said to Mary Beth, "Shop's open tonight. I'll tell you about it tomorrow. How about meeting at Our Place?"

"No. How about bringing carry-out from them instead. You won't even have to order. Just ask Gus for two of whatever the specialty is. By now Gus knows what we want to order better than we do ourselves. Besides, I don't feel like being with a lot of people and having to talk about Austin and what I did or didn't see."

Though she really didn't want to talk about Austin's death, Mary Beth was astonished that the next day, none of her students in her two afternoon classes asked any questions at all. If they had even heard about Wednesday's horrific event, they put it aside in favor of discussions about Saturday's football game or, in the case of a precious few, about the class assignments.

CHAPTER EIGHT: THURSDAY NIGHT

"Once upon a midnight dreary/while I pondered weak and weary."
  —Edgar Allan Poe

Tony arrived at Mary Beth's white frame house while it was still light. Mary Beth had been extremely lucky to find the house, first as a rental, then unexpectedly as a house for sale at a decent price. Located right on the edge of campus, it was tucked between two circa 1860s homes, architectural stars of town and gown tours. She had been sold on the house the minute she had seen it during the weekend of her first interview with Midfield College. The simple spring landscaping with strings of blue hyacinths interspersed with large clumps of yellow daffodils did more than the real estate agent to get her to sign the rental agreement.

Even with a sudden double sneeze he couldn't smother, Tony was too excited to notice the yard suddenly full of exuberant autumnal ragweed. He ran up the four steps to the newly painted-green front porch. Under one arm he held Our Place's brown carry-out bag and under the other, a bottle of celebratory, but cheap, California champagne.

With his hands full, he couldn't get to his pocket for his own key to the house, so had to bend down to ring the bell with his chin. Mary Beth must have been waiting. As soon as she opened the door, in one fell swoop, he rose—chin first, lifted the bags, and handed them to her. Without any more preface, he began to explain, "I've been planning this with Bob for two years now, Mary Best. If you were going to make a career out of Midfield, I was too. I didn't take pay for any of my overtime for those two years. All of that hard work went into equity in the shop—especially last year when you were at that writers' conference in Lakeville."

Mary Beth gave a raised fist salute, "Go, Ohio Creates!"

Though he recognized the conference name, Tony ignored her interruption, refusing to be distracted. "It wasn't only the equity I earned either. Bob was amazed at how determined I was and how much work I could do in different areas of the business. I've really got his respect. I think he and everyone else forgot that I've earned a meaningful Ph.D. and that I wasn't just a kid earning money as a bike repairman.

"There's a lot of problem solving that goes on in a repair shop, Mary Best." He looked away from her, back inside himself as he spoke.

"That is so fabulous, Tony. I'm thrilled for you. Bob's getting a good deal, too." Her lips switched muscle sets—from those that turned her lips up to those that turned them down. "I hope I still have a job at the college and don't have to leave."

"Don't worry, Mary Babe. I can always give you a job at the cash register—if we had a cash register," Tony grinned.

Mary Beth didn't. She was reminded of the cash register in AUSTIN'S Arts & Antiques.

She broke the party mood. "Now we have to find out what happened to Austin. I'm sure he was murdered. Do you want to work with me to solve this crime or not?"

"I thought you'd never ask."

"Well, let's get started. I don't know if we'll get any answers, but we can ask Seth some questions," she said as they moved into the living room and started to unpack their carry-out dinners.

"We can ask Abby. Hey, we can read *The Daily Record*, or whatever. Oh, my Lord, you haven't even heard the tape yet. We'll play it tonight."

"I'm good to go, Mary Best. The sooner we find out anything, the sooner I get myself out from under that so-called 'cloud of suspicion.' Its hovering over me is all too real."

"But, Tony, we don't even know if officially a crime was committed, even though everyone's acting as if it's a murder. I'm sure Seth must know. Unless there's an acknowledged crime, how could suspicion be hovering over you or anyone else? Anyway, you and I do know that, officially or not, there was a horrendous crime. Before we go mindlessly trying to solve it by exploring the dunes or examining cryptogenic poisons, let's make one of your famous lists of what could have happened."

"Sure. I'll start. We don't have many murders in Midfield, but those you get tangled up with sure are interesting, Mary Beth." She gave him a look.

Tony realized his error and changed tactics. "OK, here's my

first list. 1. Nothing happened. Austin died of natural causes. 2. He died of an accidental overdose."

"Good start. You take notes. I'll go on. 3. He was murdered by mistake. Someone was trying to get me."

"What?"

"Seth thinks that's a possibility. I'll tell you about it later. Let's go on with the list. 4. Someone poisoned him or killed him in some other way. 5. He committed suicide. Why? Because I was coming over for dinner." Mary Beth started to giggle. "And we were only having pizza!" She could hardly get the words out. Her giggle turned into laughter, loud laughter. Tony looked at her. He started to laugh. Neither one of them could stop. They sat down on the floor laughing. They fell over on each other laughing. Entwined, they stopped laughing.

CHAPTER NINE: SATURDAY

"Believe only half of what you see and nothing that you hear."
—Edgar Allan Poe

Saturday morning Mary Beth and Tony listened to the copy of the tape. "Un-be-lieve-able," was Tony's immediate response. This guy Nat is a real wacko. Can we find him? Has any official called the sister Sophie or whatever it is?"

"Simone," Mary Beth corrected him. "I know I should have, but anyway, it wouldn't have been an official call."

Tony interrupted, "Actually, Mary Babe, I know her name, and I want to… Oh, never mind. Let's get this straightened out first. What was that business last night about your being the intended victim? As my friend the plastic surgeon would say, 'that puts a whole new face on the crime.' If there is a crime."

"Tony, it's not funny. The one thing we know about this case is that Austin is dead. Seth pointed out that I was on the club ride when he had his bike accident and that I was due at his apartment when he had his life's final 'accident.' I'm no Zelig, honey. And Seth decidedly doesn't believe in coincidences when it comes to criminal investigations."

"Mary Best, that doesn't make any sense. Do you have enemies? I know that cold fish in your department, Hake, isn't crazy about you. Anyone can see that."

"I used to think that, too, Tony. I've come to realize that he's an equal opportunity growler, though, believe me, I'm keeping a record of his slurs at HR. Worse, he's as captious a grader of student compositions as he is of people."

"Possibly, though he seems to concentrate on you. He sees you as competition. You publish regularly; students sign up for your classes. You're a potential power he doesn't want to reckon with.

"Plus, sorry, hon, in this case, something else is going on. I doubt it, but maybe you accidentally hurt someone, physically or emotionally, someone who wants to get back at you. To put it delicately, you are prone to the occasional episode of social clumsiness.

Then it's more than a possibility that some of your students could hate you if you gave them low grades, or worse, if you flunked them. But I can't imagine that any of those people would want to kill you."

Tony stopped to re-think what he had just said. "None of them would have the guts for it. They're literature majors. I agree with Sinclair Lewis 'our American professors like their literature clear and cold and pure and very dead.' But not people!"

"I'm going to ignore that crack, Tony. It relates to me, too, you know. I've got more important things to worry about. It's going to be so weird to walk around campus, thinking 'Is that person out to get me? Or that one?' I sure hope Seth gets the victim part of this sorted out ASAP. But what can we do?"

"Austin left us with two directions to follow: the nutty Nat-guy and the thought that someone, and I know that someone is not me, so the thought that someone else out there fiddled with your bicycle that Austin was riding on that Club Ride to the Amish Inn."

"He left a third direction to follow."

"Say again."

"He left something else, that almost tattoo on his arm. Tony, I have an idea, though you'll think I'm peculiar."

Tony smiled.

Mary Beth ignored that response. "In class we're studying Poe's 'The Purloined Letter.' Here's what his detective, Monsieur Dupin, suggests for mystery solving."

She reached for her notes and read, "'If it is any point requiring reflection,' observed Dupin, as he forbore to kindle the wick, 'we shall examine it to better purpose in the dark.' Let's give it a try, Tony. Let's think in the dark. It can't hurt."

That smile appeared on Tony's face again, though he tried to squelch it.

Mary Beth didn't see his changing expressions as she was reaching for the light switch. When the lights went off, she tried to picture her mind as the whiteboard on the wall behind her desk. She erased all of the clutter. She waited. She tried not to look at Tony. They managed to sit in the dark without saying anything for five minutes, ten minutes.

"Well," she said, giving up, "let's go to Austin's art and stuff and nose around a little. Maybe we'll see something out of place or pick up some kind of a clue, even if it's ephemeral."

"You go, Mary Beth," Tony said, refraining from any comment on the Monsieur Dupin exercise. "I'm going over to Bob's, I mean," he proudly smiled, "Tony and Bob's to do some paper work. I wouldn't know what if anything was out of place at Austin's. I've only been there once before. The whole store seemed like a junk shop to me. Plus I'm sure Seth has already gone over it. But go ahead, check it out."

More practical than Mary Beth, he called for a plan of action, "We have to follow up on our two leads, three, if we count the sister Simone. No, four, if we count Austin's non-tattoo. You're right. Simone and the bicycle lead can wait. The bike won't leave the shop. I can examine it any time. I don't need to point this out," Tony added almost visibly swelling again, "but someone here knows almost everything there is to know on the subject of bicycles."

"C'mon, Tony, you don't have to tell me. I know darn well how good you are—in just about everything," she laughed.

"Thanks, Mary Babe. You're pretty good yourself. But last night was last night. Now is this morning, 'Here hath been dawning/ Another blue day/ Think, wilt thou let it/ Slip useless away?'"

With an exaggerated bow, Tony finished the quotation and added, "From Carlyle to you, Mary Beth and on to Austin and our plans. If that tattoo is a symbol, I'll be able to figure it out later. For now, let's go out to the dunes as soon as we can. Indiana's not so far away. Someone there must know something. Austin and Nat couldn't have been the only two players on that field of sand."

"That's the plan? You don't go in for detail much, do you? For starters, we both have jobs that are more than full-time. Between grading papers and faculty meetings, I don't have much of a life, let alone a second career as Mary Beth Goldberg, girl crime-fighter. How are we going to find the space in our calendars to do all of this murder solving? Let's say that you're right—again. Our over-arching plan is to follow the leads, dunes first; thereby and eventually solving the crime. That's pretty simple. We'll work out a detailed plan of time, money, and action later."

"Much later. But how's a dune trip next weekend for starters? Right now, I'm going back to work. We're overwhelmed at the shop. People are even bringing in their garage art."

"What's garage art?"

"You know, Mary Babe, all of those bicycles people have hanging on their garage walls, the way they hang paintings in their living rooms. Those are the bikes no one ever plans to use again, but can't stand to throw away. They're just decorating the walls. Customers are bringing those wrecks in to be made to look like new. Not going to happen. I hate to stand in the way of the greening of Midfield. But 'not' and 'happen' are the operative words."

Mary Beth and Tony had chatted their way down the center stair-well, opened the screen door, and were standing on the front porch. As Tony gave Mary Beth a goodbye hug, Gary Hake passed by and called to them with a knowing smile. "Hi, Mary Beth and Tony. Having a little time out from the work week, are you? I can't ever remember what it means when your people say kvelling, Mary Beth. Is it quarreling or full of pride? Either way, it seems like that's what you two were doing, among other things."

After sharing a quick, joint grimace with Tony, Mary Beth brought her meaningless, professional smile into play and pretended not to notice she was dropping books in shock at Gary's crudeness. She bent over in a well-practiced swoop to pick up the dropped items, while managing a wave to Gary, who waved back while calling out, "just kibitzing."

Books in hand, Mary Beth elaborated her anti-Hake plans. "It's hard to believe, Tony, but last week I had a meeting with Gary to address what I termed inappropriate language directed at me. Do you know what his response was?"

"Well, no, Mary Beth, I don't."

"He said to me, 'Don't be a nebbish.' I've added that to my list at HR. I'm not filing an official complaint yet, but I'll be ready with a rather robust attack, complete with documentation, the minute he steps over the line."

"Right now," Tony added, "I'm just glad he didn't stop. Go on with what you were saying."

"I'm going over to Austin's place," Mary Beth said. "Seth has the apartment cordoned off, but I'm sure I could look around the shop. I'd know if anything was disturbed. Naturally I don't know Austin's inventory, nobody could know that inventory, but I'll bet I could tell if anything had been moved by the dust marks."

"I'll bet," Tony said, "It's not the most immaculate shop in town. Austin was the type who thought a little dust added to the antique ambiance."

Mary Beth locked her front door and put the key under the doormat, where no one in the world would think of looking. She and Tony walked part way towards town together before Tony turned off for the shop. As they walked, their bodies touched in a way that caused passing neighbors and students to smile benignly.

CHAPTER TEN: SATURDAY

"Exams most foul."
—Contemporary satirical reference to *Hamlet*

When Mary Beth arrived at AUSTIN'S awesome, authentic art & antiques, she was confounded by seeing the door open. More confounding was the sight of Robby with Celeste and Liz in tow, wandering around as if they owned the place.

"Hi, Professor." said Celeste. "When we figured out how to open the door, we thought there'd be nobody near us to see us or hear us."

"What in the world are you doing here?" Mary Beth asked in her authoritative voice, a tool she used to cover her worry that they might ask her the same question. They didn't. She was still the teacher, the alpha male of their small group.

Liz answered first. "You know I used to be a roustabout with the circus."

"What?" exploded Mary Beth. If that was true, her judgment of Liz had been nowhere near the bulls-eye, in fact, completely off the target. "I thought that autobiographical essay you wrote the first day of rhetoric class was an exercise in fiction."

"Oh, no, I've been with the circus each summer since I was sixteen. I plan to go to Clown College in Florida after I graduate. Want to see me twist balloons into a hat?"

"But you're so petite."

"So?"

Mary Beth quickly swallowed another prejudice she didn't know she had and listened while Liz explained.

"I thought my roustabout experience would come in handy and I could help pack up all of Austin's stuff and earn a little spending money."

"Yeah, Professor," agreed Celeste. We wanted to get here before the deep purple falls over sleepy garden walls, and we couldn't see any more."

"I came separately," Robby answered. "I thought maybe I could find something for mom for a present and when I ran into the girls, they said they'd help. You could help more, Mary Beth. You know her pretty well. And you're about her age."

Mary Beth thought of her friend, Peggy, Robby's mom, a good ten years older than she was. *Is Robby playing games? Trying to see what he can get away with again? Or does he just see everyone over thirty as being the same age—old?*

"This is no place for students. Why don't you go back to campus, back to studying Poe? I might even give a surprise test Monday."

"I've got those short stories down cold." Robby bragged.

He probably does, Mary Beth judged. She remembered that he had written an "A" paper about Poe's short story "The Imp of the Perverse." He linked it to one of Poe's overarching themes, the doubleness of experience. Robby examined the chief protagonist in the story, a condemned murderer who had concealed his guilt for years, then following a perverse impulse, confessed. The murderer (and Poe) explains that perversity is an unrecognized major motive for people's actions.

Robby interrupted her line of thought. "I think I'm the epitome of his 'imp of the perverse.' I always do have this urge to undo my own security."

Which is exactly what you are doing right now, Robby, when your boasting tempts this teacher to test you past your knowledge, is what Mary Beth refrained from saying. What she did say was, "Scoot, the three of you."

Celeste paused to say goodbye, "You're right, Professor. I'll leave my troubles on Austin's doorstep. Then you could direct your feet to the sunny side of the street."

Mary Beth repeated her directive, "Scoot." This time they did.

With her students out of her way and philosophic questions put aside, Mary Beth studied Austin's shop. She could see that the police had been through it. In fact, the antique cash register with those perhaps-telling returned checks had been removed. The shop computer had been disconnected. Other items appeared to be exactly where they had been placed when Austin moved in a few months ago. He'd had his own logic in stocking his shelves: collectibles were toward the front, genuine antiques in the back, and perishable documents locked in his office.

Mary Beth started with the collectibles. They seemed uninteresting to her, but she was aware that Austin knew his merchandise. He had specialized in old bottles of all kinds that had been manufactured in Ohio. He wasn't as selective with the ash trays that were on the next rack. They seemed to come from all over. Mary Beth noted that Austin had been an excellent merchandiser, showing practical application of what to her were useless items. He had artistically arranged a few branches and flowers, now dead in one of the bottles, herbs in others, and laid out frilled party toothpicks in two of the ash trays. But nothing jumped out at her; nothing was labeled "clue."

She didn't have any better luck in the antique room. For all she knew Austin was passing off good reproductions as genuine antiques. Not that she'd believe that of him. He was her friend, always straight-forward. And what kind of a motive for crime would that have been? It would have been a reason for police intervention. Still, she certainly couldn't tell what was genuine.

As she moved back in the shop toward the office, Mary Beth felt she would be able to tell something about the authenticity of old documents, especially old books. *I've spent so much of my life doing research in dusty volumes, she thought. I think I'll be able to just smell the genuine article. Ha, I made a pun to myself.* She smiled at the thought, though picking through the detritus of Austin's business life was making her feel sadder with each stratum she uncovered.

The key Austin had given her only a few days earlier was the key to the two entrance doors: in from the street and from his apartment. It didn't open the office, but Mary Beth had no trouble jiggling the lock when she got to that door. *If l sit at Austin's desk in his chair, I might be able to channel him or feel his aura. It doesn't have to be pseudo-mysticism. When I sit where he sat and look where he looked, maybe something I hadn't noticed before will fall in my line of sight or maybe I can find an interesting desk top doodle—anything, maybe a repetition of the circle and line on his arm.* She sat and, in an attempt to approximate Austin's height, stretched her arms, legs, neck. Still only a mini-Austin, she tried to see what he might have seen. No interesting views in the windowless office.

The only notes on the desk top looked as if Austin had been playing the childhood game of "hangman," *so there was a desktop doodle, after all.* Austin (or *someone,* she added) had made stick figures of a hanging and a grave. *Was that a bunch of flowers next to it? Or carrots? And what were the notes? "Poo poo poo." Now when would Austin have said "poo," for Pete's sake?' He wasn't much for swearing, but he wasn't much for "poo" either. Maybe he had been entertaining a customer's child.* Mary Beth dismissed the doodling.

She looked around from what would have been his vantage point. At her right was an old bible box that Austin had used as a "do now" file cabinet. She started to go through it, looking at torn-out newspaper clipping after newspaper clipping, old bill after old bill. From the inconsistent arrangement of file entries, she had the feeling she wasn't the first to examine the box's contents. *Well, of course, Seth had been here and must have gone through things. I wonder if those three kids were in the office, too. I wouldn't put it past them.* Mary Beth wasted some time going through a file Austin had titled, "Poets and Writers." *Was he saving this information to give to me,* Mary Beth wondered as she checked out newspaper clippings, computer print-outs, and copies of old letters about Hawthorn, Melville, and Poe, the stars of her American Romantics class.

Dissatisfied with her progress, she picked up her own papers that had tumbled onto the floor and got ready to leave. *That's a "D" for the afternoon's work,* she said to herself going into her usual self-critical mode. *I wouldn't give myself an "F;" after all, I did look around. Let's call it a preliminary study! Maybe something I've seen will register later,* she thought with sincere belief in the academic workings of her subconscious. *I'll stop by to report to Seth on my way home. If I tell him I've been at the site before he finds out on his own that I've been snooping, he won't be as angry with me. I think.*

She saw him just as he was entering his office. "Sheriff, sheriff."

He turned and repeated in a resigned voice, "Just call me Seth, Mary Beth. I don't care if we're around other folks or not. I was going to call you anyway. If authentic, the tape you gave me could be a big help. I'm calling that sister, that Simone lady. Were you searching me out for anything special?"

"I wanted to tell you that I was just at Austin's shop looking around. I didn't take anything, didn't move anything. I just peaked upstairs at the apartment and saw that the area around Austin's desk was still covered in finger-print powder, so I kept away."

"I'm not interested in hearing your defense. You had no business being there. It's still a potential crime scene."

"What I wanted to tell you, Seth, is that I wasn't the first. When I got there, the odd student threesome was already investigating."

"Threesome? That's Rob, the history prof's son; the black girl who told me she likes to talk with me 'as time goes by;' and that little blond girl who was a professional parachute jumper? I agree. They are a little odd."

"Parachute-jumper? Professional? Are you talking about Liz?"

"Yep. That's her name."

"She told me she was a professional roustabout."

"Maybe she's a professional liar. One thing she is for sure, she's someone who bears re-examining."

"Seth, she's probably a complete innocent, in training to be one of the obligatory eccentrics on campus."

"Speaking of innocents, Mary Beth, I've heard you plan to go to the Indiana dunes. You and Tony have that hankering to find unicorns. I believe in checking out the ponies first. I'll stay right here at the ranch. Mind you, I can't do anything officially until I get the coroner's report, and you two shouldn't be meddling either."

CHAPTER ELEVEN: SUNDAY

"We only understand backwards, but we must live forwards."
 —Soren Kierkegaard, *Journals*, 1843

Trying to bury Seth's chastisement, Mary Beth allowed herself to sleep in, as her Ohio colleagues would say. Deep into an REM dream phase, she missed seeing the weekly parade of Sunday morning church-goers. One of her simple, small-town, Sunday pleasures was to nod to couples and families as they righteously marched past her porch.

She even missed Roger Christian, her colleague and neighbor, whose secular ritual of picking up the Sunday *New York Times* took place on a more rigid schedule than the church services he ridiculed in his role as the college's public atheist. She smiled as she remembered last Christmas. While other Midfieldians were hanging all the tinsel the town had to offer, Roger countered the decorations by hammering into the frozen earth of his summer rose garden a hand lettered sign that proclaimed, "Atheism is a non-prophet organization." No one noticed. He took it down two days later.

The teapot's whistle brought Mary Beth back to the here and now. While she brunched on a cream-cheesed bagel with ham, she resolved to spend the day, or whatever was left of it, getting something accomplished in the housekeeping department. First though, she took her second cup of Irish breakfast tea to the computer. Nothing from Gabe. But two e-mails from sylsheriff@oh.state.org. What could they be about? Cleverly figuring that the best way to find out would be to read them, she did, opening the newest e-mail first.

"Mary Beth, please immediately delete the e-mail just sent. Do not mention it to anyone. I will owe you big time. Sincerely, Syl"

He didn't even take time to spell check, she thought as she opened the earlier e-mail.

Wow. This is what he's talking about, obviously a group mailing that I'm not supposed to see. No wonder Syl wants me to delete it. I will. "After I print out a copy," she said out loud as she pressed, "print."

To those interested in the Austin Westlake case:

At the request of Sheriff Seth Yoder, I am forwarding the following private information: The autopsy results (anatomical summary, external evaluation, and clothing examination) from Dr. Abby McKenzie have been received by the sheriff's office. Nothing unusual is revealed. Although the toxicology report is not complete, unofficially we are saying that the cause of death is a poison yet to be identified. It was administered by person or persons unknown. In the absence of a note or motive for suicide, the death is being investigated as a murder. Austin's art and antique shop is therefore a crime scene. No unauthorized persons are permitted to enter the shop or apartment above it. Anyone who does enter the premises will be criminally trespassing.

Sylvester Morse

For Sheriff Seth Yoder

Tears welled up in Mary Beth's eyes as she read. Her nose ran. She reached on her desk for a tissue. She reached within herself for resolve. *How could anyone murder —murder? Yes, this makes it official. How could anyone murder—such a nice guy? Why? He seems more innocent than some of my students. I'll find out why and I'll find out who,* she promised herself and Austin. *Detecting's been sort of a game so far. It won't be any more!*

She re-read the e-mail after printing it. This time brought laughter instead of tears. *Inspector Morse indeed. More like Inspector Clouseau.*

She went back to work, first picking up some papers lying on the floor, including outdated supermarket coupons she had clipped in one of her fits of economy. She took time to shuffle her emotions back in order by shuffling books from her to-be-read-this semester pile to her to-be-read-later pile—then, back again.

She continued alternating mindless cleaning and simple grading of papers, checking topic sentences and other paragraph corrections that allowed her subconscious some space to ponder the crime. *I was at the scene,* she thought. *I would've noticed if there had been a forced entry. The murderer must have been someone Austin let in, someone he knew.*

Oh, my God! Someone I know?

CHAPTER TWELVE: MONDAY

"…Wine is constant proof that God loves us and loves to see us happy."
  —Benjamin Franklin, *The Posthumous and Other Writings*, 1819

Mary Beth put thoughts of Austin and of murder out of her mind as she dressed for class on Monday morning. Instead she concentrated on her running list of "things to worry about to-day." She knew that fussing about her Loomis Hall wardrobe was a screen to hide other anxieties (and a flutter of excitement). It was really apprehension about her appearance for her Ye Olde Gaol appointment that concerned her. *Does this tight sweater make me look too ready, even louche? It's navy blue; that's not much of a statement.* Still she toned it down by looping a long gray scarf twice around her neck. Then in a not unusual fit of mirror-doubt, she questioned the look. *Maybe I should wear a vest today. No, if anything is going to make me look safe and academic, it's this grey knitted scarf down to my knees.*

She hurried out the door with the idea of forcing an unplanned, casual meeting with Liz top front in her mind. She put the serious navy blue sweater and grey scarf problem where it belonged, at the bottom of her worry list. But no Liz greeted her at the entrance to room #301 and no Liz was seated in the class.

When questioned about her pal, Celeste said, "Oh, Liz had to make a sentimental journey home."

"What are you talking about, Celeste?"

"She had to fly home last night. Her dad was bitten by a ground-hog and died of a heart attack."

"Don't tell me she lives deep in the heart of Texas?"

"Why, Professor, how did you know? That's just what she told me."

Liz has to be stopped thought Mary Beth, though what she said was "Thank you, Celeste."

Celeste continued talking, proud to be the bearer of so much information and equally proud of the accomplishments of her best friend. "Liz is a regular cowboy. She has a saddle and spurs that jingle jangle as she rides merrily along."

Robby arrived in time to hear that line. He smiled and almost paternally shook his head as he edged Celeste into the classroom. They now sat in the back row next to the door, a section sacred to baseball players, who would rise as one to leave class early and ostentatiously for scheduled practices.

Mary Beth mentally threw up her hands in seating-plan defeat and returned to something she did know about: E.A. Poe. She assigned one of her own articles, "A Birder's Re-reading of Poe's 'Romance.'"

"Isn't that a little esoteric, Professor Mary Beth?" Robby called out.

Instead of answering Robby, Mary Beth directed her answer to the class. "We will use this study during each class session this week. I suggest you keep in mind my two purposes in asking you for a close reading of this material: to discuss the various interpretations of the poem and to emphasize the value of research. Think of these goals while you read."

A few hours later, filled with trepidation (*What if Gabe doesn't like me?*) and guilt (*What if he does?*), Mary Beth entered Ye Olde Gaol and, adding to her nervousness, had to listen to her heels clunking down the stone steps. It took her eyes a few seconds to adjust to the darkened cellar cum restaurant. Then she saw him— across a crowded room—*Celeste would love that she thought. He's even better looking than on Facebook.* She forced herself to walk over to him in a manner befitting a successful professional and, of course, tripped as she reached the table. Gabe caught her. The immediacy of the electric current between them almost frightened her. Still, she let herself be held a little longer than necessary, enjoying the rough texture of his tweed jacket and the slight smell of, *was that chlorine? Could he be a swimmer, too?*

She asked. He was. Words flowed. She could almost feel her eyes and conversation brightening with everything he said.

The waiter gave her needed time to collect herself when he brought Gabe a previously ordered drink. "Your 'Spirit Ascending,' Sir."

"Sounds more like an art object," Mary Beth responded.

"It is," Gabe smiled, taking a sip.

It wasn't until the waiter returned to take their meal order that

Mary Beth said, "By the way, I'm Mary Beth Goldberg."

He held her eyes with his while he smiled, saying, "And I'm Gabe."

"What if I'd been talking all this time to the wrong blind date?" she smiled back.

"No chance of that. I told you I know you, and I do." They couldn't stop grinning at each other. "Plus, just to be certain, I googled you. Why were you so stingy with information on Facebook?"

"I didn't want my social networking to interfere with my academic networking," was the prim reply. It was the last prim reply of a heady evening.

It wasn't so much what was said; it was what was felt. Mary Beth was constantly aware of the strong pull of tension that hovered under the surface of the most ordinary parts of their conversation. Yet the conversation was anything but ordinary to her. She was amazed when Gabe looked at his blackberry and said, "Time to go. Nine o'clock. That's tonight's pumpkin time."

"Mary Beth, something important is going on here. You must feel it too."

She acquiesced.

"It's too important for me to fool around. I'm playing by your rules now. But I'm warning you that I expect you to be playing by my rules later. Speaking of which, can you come to Cleveland Friday night, my territory this time?"

She nodded agreement.

"The Baricelli Inn, again at six. One day at a time. Let's make it one great day at a time," he added and left.

Shaken and stirred, in a most positive way, she reminded herself, Mary Beth walked home wondering what to say to Tony. Another unnecessary worry. The subject never came up. Tony had been busy at the bike show in Akron and would be there again on Saturday.

Mary Beth filled the week with work. Her classes had never been so well planned. Some would say that the spontaneity that made her such a good teacher was missing. Any free half-hour in her appointment book was filled with either a required student conference or with trying to make some sense of Austin's death. She would not give herself an unscheduled minute when she might think of Gabe.

And it was Friday.

Now she had to think of him and the evening ahead. She had to think of the potential that drove that electric current. The practical side of her won. She packed a few overnight necessities in her prized eBay find, her Coach bag. *If nothing happens, nothing happens. Gabe won't ever need to know that I brought a toothbrush along. And why am I turning into such a prude that I use euphemisms to myself? 'Toothbrush,' indeed.*

MapQuest brought her to the Baricelli Inn where Gabe was waiting at a table for two. Before she walked across the restaurant to him, she looked at her watch. *Mary Beth, the Punctual Professor, exactly on time. That sounds exciting,* she thought. *Maybe it will be,* she amended, and resolved to act more conventional than she was beginning to feel. This caused her to start the conversation with a series of pleasantries, "What a beautiful restaurant. I've heard about it, but never been here before." Her actions were in the same vein. When she sat down she carefully crossed her legs.

Then she realized what she was doing. *Come on, Mary Beth,* she said to herself, *anyone who has ever taken Psych 1 knows what that's all about.* She just as carefully uncrossed her legs and put both feet solidly on the floor.

"It really is an Inn, built as a home in 1896," Gabe was explaining. "The bed rooms are upstairs. I reserved one for you, in case you didn't want to drive back to Midfield tonight."

She looked up at him startled, thinking, *isn't that taking a lot for granted?*

He understood the look and the unspoken thought. "Mary Beth, I'm not here to cadge favors from you. If a 'favor' was all I wanted I could go to the nearest bar and meet someone who would be glad to favor me. If I tried it around Midfield College, that someone might even be one of your students.

"I'm not a kid anymore. I'm 39 and I'm looking for a serious, adult relationship. In a way, I fell for you when I heard you speak at the Cleveland Symposium on Poe. Boy, were you enthusiastic. I was immediately attracted. Then I stalked you on the Internet. I even read your paper, 'Beyond The Raven.'"

Mary Beth smiled at his hyperbole. But, *had he really read the study?*

"The next step was our e-mails. And here we are." He poured them each another generous glass of sauvignon blanc´. Mary Beth nervously drank it, glad to have something to do with her hands until dinner arrived. For the minute, she forgot how sleepy she got after a second glass of wine.

She owed Gabe a truthful answer to the question he had not directly asked. "Gabe, I have to tell you that I'm already involved in a serious relationship that has lasted a number of years now."

He interrupted. "I understand about your friend Tony. If your relationship with him was truly serious, you wouldn't be here with me now. That's all I need to know.

"We have a wonderful time together, Mary Beth."

She felt herself blushing in agreement.

"There's magnetism between us. I've asked myself, 'what's the take-away?' I've answered the question, too. We're already more than friends." He reached out and took her hand, an unimportant gesture.

Is there's such a thing as a full-body blush? At least he can't see it… right now. That thought alone increased the intensity of the telltale heat she felt rising in her cheeks. She withdrew her hand, demonstrating the intimacy inherent in that unimportant gesture.

The waiter poured more wine when he brought dinner, this time an inexpensive, but well-rounded Montepulciano from Abruzzi. He left the bottle and said, "Excuse my interrupting, Mr. James, but you might like to consider a Clan Sinclair Single malt Scotch. We just got a shipment in from Edinburgh, and I know it's your favorite." *He's been here before*, Mary Beth thought, and why not? Gabe declined with a few appropriate words.

He and Mary Beth didn't need wine or Scotch to stimulate their conversation. In fact, Mary Beth felt the conversation was moving too quickly. She tried to apply the brakes by indulging in more superficial talk. Gabe understood what she was doing and gave a sardonic smile. Mary Beth died a little. She thought of all of those high school years spent with her pals in front of mirrors trying for that same sardonic smile or the woman-of-the-world lift of an eyebrow. *But*, she remembered, *I could wiggle my ears*, which, without realizing it, she proceeded to do.

"Mary Beth, what in the world are you doing?" Gabe was laughing so hard, other diners turned to look. Mary Beth stopped wiggling her ears and turned red again.

She struggled to start a conversation she could control, "I meant to ask you, why were you at a Poe conference in the first place?"

"Mary Beth, I'm a screen writer. I think I'll put a girl wiggling her ears in my next script." He smothered a laugh. "Seriously, it's been a long time since I read Poe, but I happened to pick up a book, *Poe Poe Poe* and it reminded me of his rich store-house of stories— just waiting for me to put into contemporary settings and exploit. I saw the announcement of the conference in *The Plain Dealer.* Hey, I've picked up ideas from odder places that that."

Poe Poe Poe. Is it possible that Austin had not been writing 'poo poo poo' at his desk? When that thought popped into her mind, Mary Beth found it imperative to tell Gabe selected parts of the story of Austin's murder and her determination to find the murderer. She even told of her planned trip to the dunes to follow her main suspect. She managed to leave out the part about Tony's accompanying her.

"I hope the system of the irrelevant clue works for you," was Gabe's response. In answer to the question mark apparent on her face, he explained, I'm a screen writer, remember? That's from Ray Milland's 1948 hit, *The Big Clock* He added up all of the small, so-called irrelevant clues the police weren't following and found the killer."

Mary Beth thought of the non-tattoo. If a clue at all, it was certainly being treated as irrelevant. Happily identifying with Ray Milland (*or was that in The Lost Weekend?*), Mary Beth realized she had been sipping wine throughout the conversation. *Could it have been three glasses? Four?* She surprised herself by being the one to acknowledge the bedroom upstairs by saying that she was too tired to drive back to Midfield.

Gabe took her hand and led her through the restaurant to the narrow staircase on the other side of the Inn's entrance hall. He opened the first door at the head of the stairs. Yes, he's definitely been here before. A warning started to go off in Mary Beth's head. It was forgotten as he pulled her against him while he closed the door and her mind with a kiss that obliterated all previous kisses. The kiss and the removal of her cardigan were so sensual and so full of promise that Mary Beth found herself again frightened by this strange and wonderful man. "I have to sit down for a minute," she said. She sat down and, much to her later chagrin, fell fast-asleep.

When she awakened early morning, a blanket was over her with a note pinned to it. 'I'll call you early in the week. Next time, I manage the wine." Signed "Your G" with the word "your" underlined.

Mary Beth re-fueled with a quick breakfast of French pastries and Maharishi Ayur-Ved tea on the inn's porch. The mid-Ohio meal that managed to combine Parisian excitement with the Maharishi's promise of balance worked. She made it back to Midfield and through her Saturday conferences and meetings without any blunders—that she noticed.

CHAPTER THIRTEEN: SUNDAY

"I am on the verge of mysteries and the veil is getting thinner and thinner."
—Louis Pasteur, letter, 1851

On Sunday morning, freed from course work and bike shops, Mary Beth and Tony left in her P.T. Cruiser convertible for the Indiana Dunes State Park. With the top down and the sun so bright that sunglasses were a necessity, not just a fashion statement, the decision was made for Mary Beth to drive to and Tony to drive from.

Tony pushed his seat back as far as it would go. Stretching out, he said, "On a day like this, it's hard to believe we're on our way to solve a murder mystery, Mary Best. Especially in this metallic blue car. It almost glows in the dark and makes my soul glow with it."

"You're more poetic than usual, Tony. Any reason?"

Tony smiled.

The short first lap of their drive from Midfield to Cleveland was uneventful, as was the five hour drive, following I-90 and I-94, highways that brought them to the dunes and their destination of exit 16. It was a drive that Mary Beth needed. *This is where I belong*, she said to herself. *Isn't it? Then why do I feel so guilty?*

Tony's companionable quietness showed that he, too, needed the space and time the drive gave them.

Mary Beth pulled in at the first motel with a vacancy sign that Tony pointed out. Checking in and unpacking their back packs took all of five minutes.

"I'm faster than usual today because—and don't tell me you're not surprised—I think I forgot more things than usual."

"Like what, Mary Beth?"

"Sun screen for starters. Then a hat, though I like it when the sun gets my dirty blond hair more blond than dirty. And I guess I didn't pack a hair brush."

"I get the picture. I'm sure the motel has a notions shop or we'll find a drugstore later. Let's rock and roll now."

While he was talking, Tony took Mary Beth's newly repaired Cannondale and his vintage Raleigh (with its new Campy drive-train) off the car rack. Because they were experienced bikers, Mary Beth and Tony always preferred to ride their own bicycles, but in this case it wasn't a matter of choice. They had to bring them. When they checked the U.S. national park service web site, they found that that the dunes park had no bike rentals.

They headed for the dunes and were overwhelmed by what they saw: high sand dunes punctuated with sporadic clusters of green growth. Mary Beth marveled at the moving patterns of shadow and light, almost dancing on the dunes. She threw her arms in the air and danced in response. "My soul glows, too," she called. She rolled down a dune, and for a few minutes didn't mind the climb through the sand as she slugged her way upward again. She forgot Midfield. She forgot Cleveland. She was living in the minute. Tony joined her. They were in the zone, something she realized, when she thought about it later, *something that is happening to us with less and less frequency.*

Mary Beth brushed some of the sand out of her hair and the glow out of her soul. She read from their pamphlet. "Some of the dunes," she read out loud, "are 180 feet above lake level."

"But that's not all sand," Mary Beth pointed out as she came back to earth. "Part of that height comes from the dune grass. It must be three feet high in places."

"If it weren't for that Marram grass," Tony showed off recently acquired knowledge for her, "the dunes would be moving inland even faster than they are now. That dune grass helps to hold them in place.

"Let's do more sight-seeing and even *playing* later," was Tony's somewhat leering suggestion. "Right now, let's see that map."

Mary Beth pulled out the crude map the motel-owner-receptionist-maid had given them. After bicycling for about an hour in the almost straight line mapped for them, they arrived unannounced at their goal. The house of Austin's strange friend Nat Amster was elegantly hidden by quasi-dunes. Mary Beth's half-facetious query to Tony, "Should we play bad cop/good cop or bad cop/bad cop?" didn't need a reply.

No one answered the rings from the doorbell or their cell phones. "Let's check out the back door," Tony said. They found no signs of life there either or when they peeked into various un-curtained windows. They looked around as far as the horizon for signs of occupancy. All they could see was marram grass and jack pines that seemed to cover the dunes to the point of disappearance. No cars or other cyclists interrupted the view.

"Well, there's a wasted trip."

"No, not at all, Mary Beth. Maybe we can learn more from a neighbor than we ever would have learned from that Mr. Amster."

Back on the path they bicycled farther than they would have gone to find a neighbor in Midfield. "Does he even have a neighbor?" Mary Beth asked. "All I see are cottonwood trees. It's so odd to see them as part of the dune-land wildness," she said. "I remember them as city trees from my days at Northwestern. Look. We've found a neighbor."

"Nice house," Tony said, appraising the large two story contemporary home. The separated porches across the first floor were balanced by architecturally matching balconies on the second. Somewhat in awe of the house, they walked their bikes up the path and clanged the dog shaped door knocker. They smiled at each other as they heard reassuring sounds of scuffling. "Some one's there," Tony added.

A man opened the door calling over his shoulder, "Down, Hector."

Mary Beth and Tony locked significant glances. They could see that the frolicking dog, now alongside the man, was a golden retriever pup. Mutual eye rolls signaled the same thought, how many golden retriever pups living in the Indiana dunes are named Hector?

As she was the female and therefore the less threatening of the two strangers, Mary Beth followed their plan by taking the lead. She explained to the good looking African American at the door that they were looking for Nat Amster.

"Oh, are you a friend of the Natster's? He's away for a month. In fact, this is his dog Hector. I'm Dr. Goshay, Abe, the vet and, in this case, baby sitter for the pup. Come on in." he led them to his study where they could see various diplomas and photos of him with famous people holding dogs. They exchanged looks again. Abe's bragging wall of creds was all the proof they needed. He most assuredly was the vet. And the dog most assuredly was Hector.

Once seated and welcomed with a glass of cool pinot grigio, Tony blurted out, "I thought Mr. Amster's dog was dead. Didn't he shoot it?"

"Shoot Hector? Never. Nat's the most mild-mannered guy in the world. You couldn't be good friends of his or you wouldn't say that. Oh," Dr. Goshay said with an almost visible light bulb going on over his head, "I'll bet you're the victim of one of his wild practical jokes. Y'know I'm thinking of writing a book about Nat and his sense of humor. One chapter would be, 'The shot in the night." He gets his house guests in a position to hear what they think is a shot, then makes up a far-fetched story to go with it. So, he took you in, did he?"

Her pet murder suspect absolved, Mary Beth didn't know whether to laugh or cry.

Tony smiled weakly and said, "Austin, a friend of ours who stayed at the house, thought Mr. Amster was pretty serious"

"Really," said Dr. Goshay beaming. "I'll tell ole Nat when I see him again. He'll be thrilled. His jokes don't always work. The best one is his old newspaper trick." Abe laughed at the recollection.

"How about letting us in on the joke?" Tony asked.

"Well it doesn't sound like much, but it sure disorients people. See, Nat always has the daily newspaper lying around. What the fall guy doesn't know when he starts to read it is that Nat has substituted a five- or ten-year old section for the inside pages. It turns out nobody reads the date on each page. So this guy starts to read, kind of mentally scratching his head, trying to figure out why he forgot about a war going on or an earthquake. The worst is the ones who try to respond to what they're reading by sounding intelligently au courant!"

Looking at his guests' polite smiles, Abe Goshay added "Well, maybe you have to be there. Is there anything else I can do for you?"

"No thanks, we'll be on our way." And after polite goodbyes, they were.

"That Nat must have been trying to play the newspaper trick on Austin, too. Poor guy," Mary Beth said remembering the tape.

Tony was no longer concentrating on Austin. "Mary Beth, just because we didn't find Austin's murderer, the day's not completely a downer. We've already paid for the room; we can do some bicycling today; and, hey, let's still stay overnight even though our detecting work is done here. I'll call Bob. No problem. You go down for a drink first. Maybe I'll try to pick you up in the bar. How often do we get to make out in a motel room? You could take a shower. Forget the towel and walk into the room wearing my favorite outfit.

"We can always drive back to Midfield tomorrow morning. I don't have a Monday class until 1 o'clock."

Tony's excellent plan went just the way he thought it would.

CHAPTER FOURTEEN

"If at first you don't succeed, destroy all evidence that you tried."
—Frank Tygen

They searched the airwaves for local radio stations on the way home, but most of the time they found themselves going over and over their weekend of non-discovery. For the fourth time Tony said, "So Nat Amster doesn't seem to be a murderer after all."

"No, a little neurotic perhaps, but not criminally neurotic."

"Mary Beth, everyone is neurotic in their own way."

"His or her own way," she absent-mindedly corrected him and continued. "I agree; it's not Nat, but someone's a murderer. It makes me angry that an average Joe like Austin..." Tony gave a look that corrected her. She acknowledged it by saying, "Well, OK, maybe Austin isn't average either. But it does make me angry that a nice guy like Austin, trying to make a living, waiting to discover an original Michelangelo or a genuine unknown poem by Melville or Poe in all of that junk he collects and sells, meanwhile enjoying everything he's doing. And someone ups and kills him. The whole situation makes me angry, really, really angry."

"Mary Best, I'm not sure I completely understand your tirade. But I do agree with the emotion behind it. I'm with you. And in Austin's case I don't think we're mistaking personality for character. I do think that he is, rather was, a genuinely nice guy—but never average," he grinned.

Satisfied with Tony's assessment and commitment, Mary Beth leaned back and relaxed for part of the drive. "He loved art and literature, but he sure couldn't draw or write. Do you think we'll ever find out what he was trying to say with that clumsy non-tattoo?"

Then she remembered something else, "Tony, we forgot one of the possibilities: Was I supposed to be the prime victim for what became a wrongly attributed murder?" Tony's answer was to speed up the car as if he were trying to speed up his mental processes. The idea of being murdered does concentrate one's mind.

"Maybe I shouldn't be so dismissive of Syl," she added. "If I talk with him long enough, I'll bet I could tease some actual facts out of the misinformation he so willingly disseminates."

"It's a plan," Tony replied without enthusiasm.

As they pulled into Cleveland, Mary Beth thought of Gabe again and their future evenings together. She smiled to herself just as Tony turned to look at her. Thinking the smile was for him, he returned it, taking his arm off the steering wheel to give her a more than comradely pat.

CHAPTER FIFTEEN

"Deep into that darkness peering, long I stood there wondering, fearing…"
—Edgar Allan Poe

Back in Midfield, Mary Beth spent the next few M.C.C. days in following her newest, neatly itemized list of things to do: get academic life in order; get so-called love life in order; find out who killed Austin (*After all I'm a trained researcher. Like it or not, that's a great deal of what grad school is all about and I did very well in grad school. I ought to be just as successful in this kind of investigation*); find out if anyone wants to kill me; finish study for the New Orleans conference; and, get house cleaned. "Oh, hell," she exclaimed re-reading her list. "I might as well add, figure out why the U.S. is at war again."

First of all, she decided she'd better do something about her class. Now that Liz was back, she and Celeste had joined forces with some of their more strident classmates to protest the reading and studying of Poe's works. The signs shouting "child molester" and "incestuous" were some of the kinder banners students had posted around campus.

The anti-Poe group was led by Eleanor Diggings, the head of the campus post-feminist/post-racist society. In the faculty lounge her professors referred to Eleanor with lowered voices and knowing looks as "El from hell." Away from faculty, in the real world of McCollege, student film crews from the Communications Department followed El and her cohorts all over campus. Both groups basked in their symbiotic, if temporary, notoriety.

"Maybe it was my fault for going into Poe's biography at all." Mary Beth said directly confronting her class's protest at their next meeting on Wednesday. "Maybe I should have insisted that we take the work at face value and not look into any of its background. I certainly believe that all works have to stand on their own. I also believe that they and we are enriched by knowing something of their context, of the background of the writer. Poe did marry his cousin Virginia Clemm. That's a fact. And she was only 13 at the time. That's another fact, a fact that's obviously not exactly palatable to many of you. But you can't change history. In this course we will continue to study Poe and his influence. If there is anyone who does not wish to read the assignments because of moral or religious reasons, please come see me after class. We will substitute sermons of Jonathan Edwards with a paper due on his 'Sinners in the hands of an angry God.'"

No one came to see Professor Mary Beth after class.

She pulled down the "necropoelliac" and "Say NO to POE" posters when she saw them. Most of them had already been covered by other protest posters with their announcements of newer meetings and parades for more current causes. The furor died down as quickly as it had started.

CHAPTER SIXTEEN

"He who would distinguish the true from the false must have an adequate idea of what is true and false."
—Spinoza, *Ethics*, 1677

Much later Mary Beth learned that Seth had been busy investigating biking clues to Austin's death. "I don't see where Mary Beth and Austin trading bikes has diddley to do with Austin being murdered," he reportedly said to Syl who nodded in agreement as he did to everything Seth said. "But I know durn well that somethin's goin' on. What's this I hear about Tony goin' to bike shows in Akron once a week? Couldn't be. Keep your eye on him for me, Syl. I can smell a skunk at a garden party as well as the next man."

Seth had gone back to the bike shop where Bob was in the middle of making a used-bike sale. He waited around, thumbing through the rack of pamphlets that glowingly described potential bike trips in Ohio, the United States, and around the world. Plenty of brochures for ski resorts, too. He had enough down time to read the poster Bob had made now that eBay and other Internet sites provided competition. Bob's clever flip-chart compared the benefits and services gained from shopping at Bob and Tony's with those available when buying on-line. Experience permitted Seth to read the poster and, at the same time, watch Bob. He read under the title, "Benefits," item #1, "Provides fair price" all the way through to item #"10 "Laughs at your jokes and weeps at your sorrow" before Bob completed the sale.

"Pretty good decking of the competition," he said when Bob said goodbye to his customer and walked over to him. "Craigslist can't weep at your sorrows—yet."

"Hey, Seth. Thanks."

"Hey, Bob." They shook hands.

"I've got the frames from Austin's Maui Jims if you want them."

"What's that?"

"His sunglasses. The lenses were smashed when he fell, but I straightened out the wire frames."

"Keep 'em. What I need is information. Can you tell if the brakes were sabotaged?"

"Not from a cursory look we couldn't, so we took the bike apart. Hope we didn't destroy any evidence, but we couldn't tell if the brake cable was frayed or cut until we pulled the cable out of the casing. Looks like natural wear and tear to me." Bob lowered his voice and spoke with great confidentiality, "You should know, Seth, that I haven't told a soul about this."

"It's OK. The horse is out of the barn now, Bob, Everyone knows that Austin was murdered. Tony's off the suspect list, by the way. He was never really a contender. But we've been checkin' out a lot of people and know Tony had nothing to do with Austin's death. Tell him his crop is safe at my ranch."

"Say what?"

"He'll know what I mean."

Much later, Mary Beth did, too.

CHAPTER SEVENTEEN: LATER WEDNESDAY, OCTOBER 7, CONTINUED

"Some Things Have To Be Believed To Be Seen."
—Ralph Hodgson, 1871-1962

Mary Beth was trying to combine her avocation of detecting with her vocation of teaching and not succeeding 100% with either. "I've got to find out what's going on with Liz," she explained when she backed out of plans with Tony. She stopped her excuses after giving the Liz-alibi. She wasn't yet ready to include a discussion of her relationship with Gabe in those explanations.

She was more than ready, though, to discuss her concerns about Liz. "Maybe Liz needs help. Maybe she's a congenital liar. Maybe she's just having a good time. I'm going to try to meet with her advisor from the Chem Department, Dr. Ruppy. You know him, Ted Ruppy?"

"I thought you weren't on good terms with Ruppy, Mary Babe."

"That's true, Tony. Ted didn't like me for a while, but, lucky me, he has early onset dementia and he's completely forgotten that I'm the enemy. In fact, I'm his new favorite person. Last year he didn't want anything to do with me. This year he raves about me to everyone."

"Instead of going to his office, I'll get him to meet me for a drink at Ye Olde Gaol's bar. Since it's next to Austin's shop, I can throw in a little investigating."

"Illegal investigating," Tony reminded her.

"So don't tell."

As Mary Beth had surmised, Ted, as her new bff, was thrilled to meet with her any time, any place. At Ye Olde Gaol, they settled into the bar scene. They were the bar scene. Midfield does not attract a large crowd of afternoon public drinkers. Mary Beth sipped her sauvignon blanc while Ted relaxed over his Lake Erie brew. They smiled at each other.

"You're looking great as always, Mary Beth. Midfield is lucky to have you. So is the English Department. But I digress. You told me you wanted some information about Liz, a lovely young lady. You know she plans to be a lepidopterist like Nabokov. Very interesting for someone so young to be serious about such an esoteric career. The advantage is that she doesn't need any formal training, the way I did to earn all of my chemistry awards."

No more esoteric than being a roustabout or parachute jumper, Mary Beth thought.

She decided she would wait a few days before telling Ted all she knew.

Beer and wine long drained and some Liz-type information exchanged, they were ready to say goodbye. Ted left as the bartender brought the check. She called after him, "Ted, I'll pay for your drink. Why don't you leave the tip?" Her voice trailed. He was out the door.

She stepped outside, putting on her Oakleys against the remembrance-of-summer sun and... *is that Ted returning? I shouldn't have judged so hastily* she mistakenly said to herself.

Ted wasn't returning to pay for drinks. "Wow, one man with selective dementia," she texted Tony.

When she started listening to Ted again, he was mid-explanation and surprisingly on-task about the reason for his return: "Mary Beth, we're right next door to Austin's shop. I know he was murdered. I'm just as curious as the next fellow. More so. Look at all of my chemistry awards," he reminded her again. "I earned those because I was willing to take intellectual risks. I'm ready for some detecting ones. I'd like to look around."

Maybe I can use him. "We're not supposed to go in, but let's," she replied, letting him take the lead in what she had planned to do all along. *Now, if we're caught, it's Ted's fault.*

As they turned toward AUSTIN'S art and antique shop, Mary Beth could see the unmistakable backs of Robby, Liz, and Celeste. The three students were facing the display window, taking turns pointing out items to the newest member of Robby's harem, El from Hell.

"This is really odd," she whispered to Ted before alerting the small band of students to her presence.

"What are you four kids doing hanging around a crime scene?"

Ignoring the "crime scene" part of the question and responding only to Mary Beth's noticing that the students were now a quartet, Celeste's unexpected reply was, "This I'll tell you, brother, you can't have one without the other."

Ted started to sing in his creaky baritone, "Love and marriage, Love and marriage, go together like a horse and carriage…"

"Stop it, Ted, Celeste, all of you. What's going on? Something's more than a little out of whack here."

"Professor, what's a 'whack?'" was Celeste's predictable response.

Mary Beth stopped herself from saying, "Someone ought to give you a good one" when she realized that Celeste was genuinely trying to improve her vocabulary.

The four truants shared guilty glances and fled.

Ted stopped singing but continued to smile benignly after the students, while Mary Beth, not thinking to use Austin's apartment key, tried unsuccessfully to enter the locked storefront. Without changing expression, Ted said, "I know I've gotten somewhat forgetful, but there are some things a boy never forgets." With that statement, he pulled a Swiss army knife with a pick, a small file, and other miniature tools out of his pocket and proceeded to open the door. As they entered, Mary Beth started to explain with gestures the lay-out of the shop. Her second dramatic throwing out of the arms to demonstrate something that had been readily apparent without her emphasis made contact with Austin's shelf of collectible glass bottles. "Ohhh." She sank to the floor with the bottles. They landed on a rubber pad. She didn't. Nothing broke in Mary Beth or the bottles, but papers fluttered from her as herbs, or leaves and twigs that looked like herbs, were disgorged by the bottles.

At that moment, Deputy Syl walked in. Right on cue. Mary Beth felt as if she were an actor in a bad senior high school play— especially since Ted was trying hard not to laugh at her unplanned slap-stick routine. She and Ted scrambled to their feet, ready to face recriminations.

"Work with me here, people. I've got murders to solve." Syl was not happy to see them.

Might as well be hanged for a sheep as a lamb or is it a goat? Mary Beth encouraged and discouraged herself, as she added, *It's only Syl.* She leaped ahead of what anyone was thinking, asking, "Syl, should I be more careful? Is the sheriff's department still considering the possibility that I might have been the intended victim?"

Ted was more startled than Syl at her questions. He had not heard (or if he had, he'd forgotten) that anyone but Austin was the intended victim. He stopped listening, making good use of his symptoms.

Syl tried his steely-eyed gaze on Mary Beth. He practiced it daily along with his bad-guy snarl and was happy to try it out. "Mary Beth, you know you have to get that information from official sources," he said looking at her for as long as he could hold her eyes.

"Syl, you are official sources," Mary Beth shot back at him.

"Yes, I am," he said as he sucked in his gut and surreptitiously polished his Elvis-buckle with his uniform sleeve.

Ted, who had already absented himself mentally, then absented himself physically from any possible conflict by kneeling on the floor to pick up bits of leaves and herbs, sniffing them, sniffing the jars, and placing the right dried material in the right bottle. The dried flowers were easy, though perhaps not as artfully displayed as when Austin had arranged them. Ted didn't need to take samples back to the lab to identify sage, mint, thyme, and other basic herbs that he grew in his own kitchen garden, though he did need occasional sips from his water bottle to cleanse his palate from the onslaught of odors. The herbs he couldn't easily identify went into the remaining empty jars to be put back on the shelf.

Mary Beth noticed what no one else did. She and Ted exchanged winks as she watched him (with more stealth than needed) stuff his pockets full of sample leaves for later study. He sauntered out.

Syl noticed Ted's leaving, but was too intent on being the font of detective knowledge to care. "Well, Professor Mary Beth," he said, "the long story is very complicated, very technical. You'll have to come down to Sheriff Seth's office and see diagrams of the bicycles in question. You'll have to read some materials on brakes, too. It's much too complicated, too technical (did I say that already?) for me to explain right now."

"*Or ever*," Mary Beth carefully did not add. She held her tongue, counted to ten, and smiled. "OK, I'll talk with the sheriff about the long story. What about the short story, Syl?"

"At this point in time, we, that is the sheriff and I, think and have discussed fully the fact or the fact, as we know it, is or appears to be that your friend; that is, not to imply anything more than a casual and platonic friendship between you and Austin. Where was I?"

"Yes, where were you? Am I a potential victim here?"

"Before I was so rudely interrupted, Ma'am, I was going to say that seeing that Austin Westlake was specifically targeted, and that he seems to be the only object of the crime. We do believe that he is the only intended object and that you are not important to this case at all." Syl stalked away.

Mary Beth sat down heavily at Austin's desk, temporarily relieved that she wasn't a potential victim and equally overcome by Syl's gratuitous insult. She wasn't so overcome that she forgot to make a new list of things to do. She pulled over a pad from top of the desk and wrote herself a note to check out the three, now four students, who were always coincidentally hanging around the scene of the murder. *Appearances aren't always deceiving,* she said to herself. *They would be an odd couple if there were just two of them, odder still with four.* Her mind meandered to the Solomonic relationship Robby seemed to have with the three young women. *Did he divide his time with Liz on Monday and Wednesday, Celeste on Tuesday and Thursday, and El for hell-raising weekends? Never in Midfield,* she reasoned.

She looked at her list. She had written on Austin's 'poo, poo, poo' pad. She looked more closely. She opened the drawer and searched until she found a magnifying glass. She looked closer still. Under magnification, it was obvious that Austin had written "poe, poe, poe." *Now what did that mean? Were Austin and Gabe reading the same book? It wouldn't even be a coincidence. I bet if I went to Amazon, I'd see that thousands and thousands of those books have been sold.*

She didn't have time to think through her ideas. Seth appeared, following up on Sylvester's call about the strange situation. He stood over Mary Beth with a hard look on his face. "What are you doing here tampering with evidence?"

"I can explain."

"I'm almost sure you can."

"Sheriff Seth," she began.

"Just call me Seth," he said wearily. "I'm not even sure I want to hear your reasoning. Try to remember, if it looks like evidence, if it walks like evidence, and if it talks like evidence, it is evidence. Leave it alone. Now hand over the pad you took from the desk."

"What's this? Poe?" he asked of no one. "It's Austin's hand all right."

"Let's call it a day here, Mary Beth." Seth waited until she was gone and secured the premises against further intrusions.

CHAPTER EIGHTEEN

"It is by presence of mind in untried emergencies that the natural metal of a man [or woman] is tested."
—James Russell Lowell, "Abraham Lincoln," 1864

Mary Beth could swear that she had just fallen asleep when an almost familiar ring woke her up. Dazed, she couldn't quite put her finger on what gadget was ringing. In a sleep-filled mutter she complained, "I hate them all, all of those machines yelling at me." She mentally filed through her noisy machine catalogue while the ringing continued. *Alarm clock? Too early. Smoke alarm? No smell. Washer or dryer? I was too tired last night. Cell?* She fumbled for the land line on the table next to her bed. She had guessed correctly. Now she could go back to sleep.

No, Seth was the caller.

"Get over here right away, Mary Beth."

"Seth it's the middle of the night. I just went to bed."

"One, Mary Beth, it's 6 a.m. Look out of your window. And two. I don't care what time it is, this is an emergency."

Aware that he meant it, Mary Beth all but stood up and saluted. "Yes, sir." She hung up. She started to brush her teeth when she realized that she had forgotten to ask something. It took a few more minutes to find her cell phone and check its directory for his number. When she reached Seth, she didn't waste any more time with her question: "Where is 'here'?"

"At Ted's house on Burbank Street."

"Why Ted's? Is he OK?"

"Mary Beth, if I called because I wanted to chat, I would've called later in the day. Get yourself over here. And, yes, it's about Ted. So move it."

Mary Beth threw on her jeans and a t-shirt and left with her hair still sleep-tousled. Worried about the new on-street parking law, she took the extra fifteen minutes she needed to bike instead of drive, spending most of that fifteen minutes mentally writing horror scripts of what could have happened.

She arrived just as the ambulance was pulling away. No sirens. A favorable sign. She left her bike on the side of Ted's drive and ran to the house. Entering the stately colonial, first between the pillars, then through the open front door with its Preservation Society seal of approval plaque, she saw on her right activity in Ted's study. Seth, Syl and Abby were gathered around Ted's desk with their backs to the hall and to her. Seth heard her footsteps and turned. His usual laid back expression was gone, replaced by one of anger and frustration. He walked into the entrance hall to meet her, closing the door of the study behind him. "Sit down for a minute in the kitchen, Mary Beth," he said leading her to the back of the house.

"What's the matter?" she asked as she pulled over the nearest antique, but comfortable, wooden chair.

"Ted has been attacked."

Mary Beth blanched and started to slide down in her chair. Seth reached out and grabbed her arm. "Mary Beth, stop," he commanded.

Mary Beth sat up straight. It had been such a modest slide that she hadn't even left the chair.

"Ted's OK. Well, almost OK," he amended. "I need you to rope yourself in. Take a few deep breaths and listen to me. I asked you to come here for two reasons: First, Ted needs you. He doesn't have any family in town, and I know you're friends. Second, I need you. This time I really want your help. That means you'll have to be sharp."

"Of course, Seth. What can I do? Just tell me, is Ted here? Does he have to be hospitalized? Why was he attacked? Was anything stolen? I'm a jinx. Something happens to everyone I talk with."

"Whoa, Mary Beth. It's not about you, and I'll ask the questions. The only thing you have to know now is that Ted will be fine, or as fine as he gets. Right now, Dr. Abby is with him in his study where he was attacked.

"I understand that you were with Ted yesterday afternoon? Right?"

"Yes, we had a drink at Ye Olde Gaol and went over to Austin's. Then your assistant Syl came and said buzz off, so Ted buzzed off."

"Did you see anyone else?"

"Only the bartender and oh, yes, that group of kids that's always hanging around the crime scene."

"You mean Robby and his two girl friends?"

"Now there are three. He's added the one they call 'El from hell.' She's got dyed black hair, with a zig-zag part on the left. She's not bad, just stridently aggressive. I chased them away as soon as we got there."

"Think. Mary Beth. Anyone else? Violent crime is so unusual around here; we're trying to figure out if there is any connection between the two attacks, if we have one unsub or two."

"Unsub?"

"Unknown subject of the investigation. Maybe it would help Ted remember what happened if he saw you again. I'll ask Abby if she thinks he's strong enough."

Mary Beth waited a few moments in the kitchen, wondering how she should approach Ted, an unnecessary worry. He had forgotten the attack.

When Seth led her into the room, Ted seemed to be askew physically as well as mentally. He leaned in one direction, his desk chair in another. He incongruously greeted her with a smile and the kind of social conversation saved for faculty teas, "Good to see you, Mary Beth. Please excuse the mess. I'm not quite sure how it happened. I'll tidy up after these gentlemen leave. My awards need straightening."

Mary Beth looked around. It looked more like her office than Ted's usually immaculate work space. Papers were scattered on the floor, and some samples Ted must have been working with were tilted, spilling contents.

Trying to jog his memory, Mary Beth said, "I enjoyed being with you yesterday, Ted."

"Yes, any time you want to go out for a drink, I'll be your date," he replied, surprising her with how much he remembered.

"Y'know, Mary Beth, I came back home after that. No, I went with you to Austin's, then I came home," he reminded himself with some effort. "It's so odd, I don't remember much. Well," he laughed "I usually don't, and that knock on the head when I fell down didn't help. But something odd happened. Yes. I do remember the pizza delivery man had a big moustache just like an Italian in a cartoon. I guess that would be a politically incorrect remark to make, so strike it. I didn't remember ordering the pizza. He said I did. I knew he must be right. Everyone else always is. Except then I remembered that I have lactose intolerance. I never eat pizza. I never order it. I don't know. I simply don't remember."

Dr. Abby interrupted, first addressing Seth, then Mary Beth. "Seth, it seems to me that Ted's memory about this incident, not about anything else," she hastened to assure him, "that his memory is coming back."

She turned, "Mary Beth, I don't believe Ted has a concussion. It seems to be only a slight bruise. I'd like to apply some kind of an ice pack. Just in case, it is a concussion, I do not want him to go to sleep for an hour or so. Would you sit with him, say until nine o'clock to make sure he stays awake?"

"Of course." Nurse Mary Beth was left in charge of the patient, obediently holding a package of frozen peas to his head. Abby and Seth, followed by Syl, who wisely hadn't had much to say, left. Mary Beth made breakfast for Ted and her, and read to him from one of his chemistry books. To keep him awake, she read words and formulas she didn't understand and couldn't pronounce. Ted was so happy for the company that he didn't bother to correct her errors or make conversation until she said, "It's time for me to leave to get ready for class, Ted. Dr. Abby said you'd be fine by yourself."

"It was almost worth getting hit on the head to see you again, Mary Beth. Have a nice day," he beamed at her. "Don't take any unordered pizzas." He laughed, pleased with himself and his narrowing world.

Later that day, she reported her uneventful morning to Seth, who brought her up to date on the investigation. "I've already interviewed the bartender on the phone. He has no connection with the case. He confirms your story that you and Ted were alone in the bar yesterday afternoon.

"I'll talk with the four students after I clear it with administration. I don't want to be sued any more than the college does. I think it will be OK if we meet as a group and in neutral territory, say the office of the Dean of Students."

Which is what they did.

CHAPTER NINETEEN

"If an eloquent speaker speaks not the truth, is there a more horrid
kind of object in creation?"
—Thomas Carlyle

After the quickly arranged interview that included Mary Beth,
Seth, and Dean Caroline Mossberg, it was decided that the
four students were just being kids looking for excitement in a small
town. No one said anything, but it was understood that any possible
connection of a Midfield College Campus student with the crime
would be swept under the carpet—again. M.C.C had to preserve
one of its chief selling points, its closeness to safe, small-town life.

On the way out of the Dean's office, Seth said to Mary Beth,
"I found your student Liz particularly fascinating because of her
interest in forensic dermatoglyphics. At that, Mary Beth rolled her
eyes and asked, "Did Liz mention circus roustabouts or parachute
jumping or lepidopterists?"

"No, why should she?" Seth answered. She's gonna come to
the office and Syl's gonna show her our finger printing equipment.
I don't know why the leader guy, Robby, thought she was funny
when she talked about her interest. She's pretty knowledgeable,
considering."

"I'll talk with the chair of the English department about her,"
Mary Beth said as they passed the cluster of grey stone science
buildings. "Or maybe I won't. I have good reasons not to," she argued, talking more to herself than to Seth. "Liz has all of these obscure careers she tells people she's interested in. So what? It must
be a minor character flaw with nothing to do with Austin's death.
My problems are really with Gary," she continued, trying to give
more reasons to keep out of the situation. "I hate to go into that office, even though I can't claim distance as a problem, the way I did
when my office was in the basement of the library. Now my office
is right next to his in Loomis. Just hearing his footsteps coming toward my office makes me feel as if I'll be attacked for some horrible,
unknown error. I'm documenting those attacks, Seth.

"So, I ask myself, why should I waste my time and end up feeling lousy just to look into the stories a happily neurotic girl is spreading about herself?

"Because the whole thing is too odd to leave alone," she answered herself, cutting off a presumed reply by Seth.

While Mary Beth argued back and forth, she and Seth had crossed campus and arrived at the entrance to Loomis Hall that faces the residential quadrangles. The quads were McCollege's successful salute to the 19th century, adding an Oxbridge touch to the Midwest school. Mary Beth found her own pro-discussion arguments convincing. Facing the fact that she had to talk with Gary, she said goodbye to Seth, who had not been listening to one word of her monolithic reasoning.

This did not keep Mary Beth from continuing her monologue, now to herself as she climbed the steps to the English Department's corridor. *Hake is the kind of egoist who is always me-deep in conversation, she thought. It'll take time and some Socratic questioning to get any information from him. But something peculiar is going on with Liz, something between trying to act out a long running joke and having a serious neurosis. It will be worth spending some time with Gary.* With that thought, she tripped on the stair runner and dropped a series of freshman comp. essays. "I'm glad there's no one watching this from the psych department," she said out loud while she picked up the scattered papers. "My body's answer to my emotional need for delay is obvious, even to me."

She continued to plan her interview with Hake, *He makes it his business to know everything that's going on at McCollege. Knowledge is power and he has plenty of both. Still early in the morning. Maybe I can catch him before class.* She ran up the remaining steps.

Mary Beth found Professor Gary Hake at his desk, which was two generations of office furniture newer than hers was, she noted, not for the first time. He was doing what he did best, happily red-inking papers. He looked up as she entered the office.

Uh, oh, here it comes, she thought. Sure enough.

"Hi, Professor Goldberg. How's your cousin Whoopi?"

She ignored Gary's idea of a joke, a joke that wasn't getting any better with repetition. In fact, she dropped all of her previous planning and didn't try to enter the conversation with a proper segue or even a proper "good morning." Instead, she abruptly said, "We have to talk, Gary. We have to talk about Liz..."

"Sure, Mary Beth. It's always nice kibitzing with you. Let me find Liz's file." While opening student files with various computer keys, he said, "She's no longer an English major, so I moved her file, but I still keep up with her. A good student and an interesting young lady."

"Interesting or wacky?"

"Interesting, Mary Beth. Did you know that she's writing an e-epistolary novel?"

"Did you know that she's a serial liar?"

"Mary Beth, what's gotten into you? Are you talking about Liz's changing her major field? Most kid change their majors a number of times."

"Oh, speak of the devil, as you like to think of her. Here's a new e-mail in the file that just came in from her. She's asking for a letter of recommendation. Of course. It must have something to do with the e-novel she was telling me about."

"Are you sure?"

"What?" He read aloud, "She says she is applying for a winter break internship at The Avian Cognition and Language Lab in Boston.

"Get outta town!" he exclaimed as he became aware of what he was reading. "Mary Beth, it's unusual for you to have such insight, but I think *this time* you're not meshugenah. She is.

"You ought to talk with her, Mary Beth. It should be a woman. Maybe you can chart those odd ambitions. Maybe she comes out with something like that once a month. She wouldn't want to talk with me about it, even though, oy vey, do I know women have problems."

Mary Beth couldn't decide which was worse, Hake's inappropriate yiddishisms, his horrible sexism, or his unsubtle reference to conflict with his live-in girlfriend from the French Department.

"I'll get you some copies of her pertinent records and you do it."

"Gary, first, I should speak with Doctor Abby about her. In fact, now that I say it, I'm sure that Abby should be the one who talks with her."

Satisfied that she now knew who to consult about Liz, that the potential problem would be out of her hands, Mary Beth left

Gary's office. As she closed the door behind her, she said, "Ciao, and if saying I wasn't meshugenah was a compliment, Gary, thanks."

He called out, "I said this time you're not meshugenah."

CHAPTER TWENTY

"It will be found, in fact, that the ingenious are always fanciful, and the truly imaginative never otherwise than analytic."
—Edgar Allan Poe

Mary Beth hurried over to her classroom. She liked arriving early. She liked the feeling of the empty classroom, the smell of it, the echoing voices of half-remembered students. She was new enough at teaching to still be excited at the anticipation of original interpretive readings, good discussions, the always present possibility that some flash of insight would enliven a student's day—or hers.

After all that had happened, this Thursday, she was especially pleased at being early and having time to set-up an exercise to illustrate Poe's cleverness and influence as a writer of detective stories. She planned to have the students take the role of his cerebral detective, C. August Dupin, and solve a Professor Goldberg-created mystery with "The Purloined Letter Approach."

The assignment for today's class had been to read the short story, "The Purloined Letter." She had explained earlier that the story was published in 1844 and was the third of Poe's three detective stories featuring the fictional Monsieur Dupin. Anyone who had read the assignment would have no problem with Mary Beth's detecting exercise. *A good way*, she congratulated herself, *to find out who has done the homework and who hasn't.*

Instead of the letter which Dupin so cleverly discovers in the story, her plan was to have the students search the classroom for a planted copy of the short story itself.

This is so much fun she thought as she surveyed the room. The set-up was perfect. Her desk was in the front of the room. Usually she stood in front of it, so the desk wouldn't present a barrier in her interaction with students. Today, though, she sat behind it, trying to put herself out of the picture. Facing the desk were three rough circles, each made up of six or seven unevenly placed chairs. Along the left side of the room was a long table, piled high with suggested resource materials that were usually ignored until term papers were due. Windows to the quad lined the right hand side. She hid the book.

Just in the nick of time. Students were entering. The fearless foursome, led the way, headed by El, with her almost painted-black hair parted on the right. She proudly wore a t-shirt left over from the protest. The slogan across her chest, "Hell no, Poe must go," was superimposed on a picture of a black raven, the international literary symbol for Poe.

Mary Beth smiled in recognition.

Three members of MCC's baseball team showed their readiness for detective work by sporting deer stalker hats. "Not Poe's headgear," Mary Beth laughed, "But the hats are more appropriate than you expected. Sir Arthur Conan Doyle was highly influenced by Poe in his creation of Sherlock Holmes, a detective who thinks his way to a solution. Now you try it."

As the students divided themselves into five teams and started to search, it was easy for Mary Beth to tell who had read the assignment and who had not. She was delighted because it seemed as if almost everyone had done the homework. Most of the small groups commandeered chairs, where they sat, looked around the room, thought for a few minutes and conferred with team mates. Only a few students started to look under the desk or asked if they were supposed to search the closet. Anyone who had read the short story would know Dupin's point: a good place to hide something is in plain sight.

She smiled in appreciation as she noted Robby and the girls checking out the coat rack. "Good readers," she said to them, acknowledging that Poe had placed his "purloined letter" on a rack of letters, what else? This made the search of a coat rack a darn good guess. But it was the three baseball players who after a careful conference bee-lined it to the table of books and found *Poe's Collected Short Stories*, opened to "The Purloined Letter."

"We wouldn't be division champs if we didn't know how to work together," Bill the captain, bragged to his professor and classmates.

Mary Beth ended class with the assignment, "Bring your favorite Poe short story or essay for tomorrow. Be ready to explain why it's your favorite. Look at this as a pre-writing exercise for an essay due next week on the same subject."

After class she went over to the bike shop for a previously arranged evening meeting with Tony, who could be found in the same cement floored, bike repair area, he had inhabited before becoming partner. Now he called it his office. New position aside, he continued to cover his black jeans and t-shirt with his old, oil stained black apron. Now he called it his uniform.

After a perfunctory, arms-length, greeting that protected Mary Beth from the apron, the two compared notes. Neither one had heard anything either officially or unofficially about any progress in solving Austin's murder. Their eyes met in agreement. Mary Beth was the first to say it, "You know we can't keep on waiting for their methodical approach to solve this mystery. Austin's just getting deader each day." She began to cry.

"There, There," Tony said, holding her in his arms, oil and all. "Don't cry, Mary Babe. I like to think of you as being perky—eternally perky."

He had the knack of making her smile, though Tony could be as serious as she was. "I know how close you were to Austin. I have the feeling, too, that we should be doing something concrete."

"Y'know what, Tony," Mary Beth said as she wiped her tears away with the sleeve of her navy blue cardigan and moved into attack mode, "yesterday we started to talk about making one of your famous lists. I think you should do it. How about a suspect list?"

Tony quickly decided not to mention the navy fuzz now under Mary Beth's eyes. He concentrated on her statement of action "Good idea," he replied, "But it needs one correction. I think WE should make one of OUR famous suspect lists."

"Of course, you're right. Let's start by your writing names on a graph. There's a chance to use that engineering background," she laughed. "The problem is that we don't really have any suspects. What do you think of Nat Amster?"

"I think he's a practical joker who we've 100% cleared, but it'll give me a name to start with. Then I'm going to add those three, make it four, kids who are always hanging around the scene of the crime. There's something odd about them, though it doesn't make them a gang of murderers."

"What about Dr. Guppy?"

"Ted?"

"Yes, your friend, Ted. Maybe all of that dementia is an act. It seems to come in handy when he needs it."

He showed her what he had written:

Suspects
Nat Amster
El from Hell
Liz
Celeste
Robby
Ted Guppy

"That's a pitiful list of suspects, Tony."

"I'll admit it's not a graph. How about if I add a column about why we think the six of them are suspects? We could call it 'suspicious acts'."

"Well, Nat said he would kill Austin. That's certainly a suspicious act."

"Yes, and Nat has a reputation as a terrible practical joker. You heard that neighbor doctor, Abe Goshay, say that people who don't like his idea of humor call him 'the g'Nat' because he's such a pest. He might be a pest, a pretty clever one, I think, but he's no suspect, even though the sister thought he was odd as far back as college."

"What about those four kids who have broken into Austin's shop three or four times that we know of? That couldn't be simply normal curiosity."

"What about Professor Guppy? He stole herb samples from the shop."

"Are you sure?"

"I saw him. I didn't think it was important at the time. He was just picking up leaves and stuff and absent-mindedly sticking them in his pocket. It's the kind of thing he would do. I still don't think it's important."

"That's it. He gets away with murder." He realized what he had said before she did.

"Hon, please don't get upset again. I didn't mean to say that. But anything the least off-beat he does gets attributed immediately to his dementia. We don't even know he was really attacked. He could have fallen, hit his head, and woven it into his alibi."

"An alibi for what, Tony? The attack real or not happened after the murder, and that is terribly real. Enough. Let's see your new list. Maybe it will help."

"Here it is, Babe, heading and all."

F.Y.I., M.B.
It's as easy as a, b, c, d
Anthony Bartlett's Clue Directory

Suspects	Reason for Suspicion	Alibi
Nat Amster	said would kill Austin, practical joker	neighbor
El from Hell	broke into Austin's shop	
Liz	broke into Austin's shop	
Celeste	broke into Austin's shop	
Robby	broke into Austin's shop	
Ted Guppy	stole evidence	also a victim
Simone, the sister	a long shot	in Akron at the time

Mary Beth didn't bother to hide her smile, as she checked the list, but she was deadly serious when she spoke. "As you said, we have a pitiful list of suspects, and worse, we have no motive for any one of them. We have to think about each suspect. In class right now we're studying 'The Purloined Letter.' Poe makes the point," she stammered, remembering that it was Gabe who had noticed this. She added, "Poe says that in solving a crime, the answer might be so simple that it is difficult. I think it's obvious that one of our suspects wanted something from Austin, something the suspect believed Austin kept in his shop. We keep returning to that shop as the center of suspicious activity."

"I think we should interview all suspects. It's worked for us before. We might uncover a motive while talking with them about something else, anything else. Just by getting them to talk. They'll say things to us they would never say to Seth or, God forbid, to Syl. I also think we can discount the Natster. Even though he's first on my list, let's leave him to the desperate end to interview only if we don't find clues through interviewing the other suspects."

"Tony, I think we should be careful to interview each one of those kids separately. They'll want to talk with us as a group. They'll protect each other."

"I agree. You're kicking the can in the right direction there."

"One other thing. I think we ought to tell Seth we're making some inquiries on our own. We don't have to go into detail, but CYA, cover your ass, is the most important thing I've learned at MCC. Sometimes I think that some of my colleagues spend more time in blame avoidance activities than they do in teaching. Maybe they have to."

CHAPTER TWENTY-ONE

"It is no easy task to pick one's way from truth to truth through besetting errors."
—Peter Mere Latham, *Collected Works*, 1789-1875

Mary Beth acted on her own advice. She stopped by Seth's office early the next morning, greeting him with a bag of bagels and a thermos of non-police-department coffee, *not a bribe* she assured herself, *a peace offering*.

"Thanks, Mary Beth. I was going to call you. I want you to sit down and listen to me. I'm even going to stop yee-hawing around," Seth said with a self-deprecating smile. "I know this is the second time we've had this conversation, but it's my responsibility to talk seriously to you.

"First of all, you should know that those four kids got a clean bill of health. Everyone in this investigation gets a clean bill of health. Everyone is innocent.

"But someone killed Austin. I think that the same someone attacked Ted Guppy. Both of those men are, were, good friends of yours. That unknown attacker could easily think that you have whatever it is he's looking for. It stands to reason that without even trying, you could be deep in the manure pile."

Troubled by Seth's seriousness, Mary Beth asked, "Did you find anything in Austin's e-mail or files or anything on his cell phone that would lead you to believe that?"

"It's not that simple, Mary Beth. We don't have a bread-crumb trail of computer calls that leads to you as a victim or to anyone as a possible murderer."

"I'm not asking you to give me secret information, Seth, but if supposedly my life is in danger, don't you think I should know what evidence makes you think so?"

"Well, I can give you more circumstantial evidence that links the Ted Guppy attack with the Austin Westlake murder. That should help you. Right here on my desk is Dr. Abby's report that the examination of stomach contents has been completed. The still unknown poison that killed Austin was delivered by means of what looks like pizza."

Pizza! Mary Beth's body absorbed the information before her mind did. She started to leap from her chair in recognition of what had been said. She almost shouted, "Ted Guppy talked about the pizza man, too."

Just as quickly she sat back down and contradicted her association of both men with pizza and crime. "Everyone eats pizza. What could that mean? It could mean nothing."

"It could mean something," Seth said quietly. "There's no record on Austin's cell phone of a call to a pizza shop, so he probably did not put in an order for one. I can't believe he would have stopped at a fast-food place for a mid-afternoon pizza snack when he knew you were bringing some over for dinner. Somewhere along the line, someone gave him some pizza. I'm going to guess, some heavily laced pizza."

"Could it have been a pizza man with a big moustache, the one Ted described before he remembered he can't eat cheese? Sorry. I shouldn't tease about it. I wouldn't like it if you did."

"Well, you could even be right, if it was a genuine moustache. I doubt that Austin would have been as easily fooled by a fake as Dr. Guppy would be."

"Thank you, Seth. I appreciate everything you're telling me. I know you wouldn't horse around with me, if you'll excuse my stealing one of your down-on-the-farm lines."

Mary Beth left the office, completely forgetting in her anxiety to mention the planned interviews of suspects, the reason she had stopped by to see Seth in the first place.

At the end of the afternoon when she met with Tony in the Student Lounge for a life-affirming cup of tea, she reported her conversation with Seth. She concluded, "It's time to get rolling, Tony. If Seth is right, my self-preservation is another good reason to find Austin's killer as fast as we can.

"I'd like our student interviews to look like spontaneous conversations. I'll go over to the library now to see if I can find one of the fearless foursome alone and studying. It's highly unlikely, but worth a try."

After a brief search of carrels and computers, Mary Beth lucked upon Celeste in the reference room. Celeste looked more earnest than usual. She had pulled back her hair so that her small hoop earrings glinted as she studiously took notes from a book on American idioms and their uses. She stood up when Mary Beth entered the room, reflecting her Zambian heritage of respect for others, especially the teacher. "Hello, Professor, I'm trying to become more verbally acclimated." She held up her reference book as proof.

"Did you know that last year, I left my village in Mwinilunga to study on a scholarship at Evelyn Hone University in the capitol? That's where I was going to learn real English. When I got to Lusaca, there was no scholarship money. Not a 100 kwacha bill to be had. They had no money to fix the broken windows or even to pay the professors. Those few who had horded kwachas found them worthless; inflation was so bad. In a month the university was closed. I was lucky to get another scholarship to come to the United States. Your Mr. Newman from the Cultural Center and Mr. Abdon Yezi from the University arranged it. But that means I've never had a chance to take English as a Second Language. I learned a lot from listening to songs on the radio. Now I'm learning much more from my friends and books like this."

"Celeste, you should be proud of the progress you've made with your English. I'm glad I *ran into* you, speaking of idioms. I wanted to ask you some questions about the day Austin Westlake was killed."

First, Celeste carefully wrote in her notebook "ran into you," then she answered Mary Beth's questions. "I don't know anything, but if there is any way I can help, I will. After all, the fundamental things apply. Have you talked with my two best friends and my fiancé?"

"We will." Mary Beth did a slow playback "What did you say? Your fiancé?"

"Yes, Robby and I are engaged."

"You're too young," Mary Beth blurted out.

"Sorry. I shouldn't have said that." She continued her thought in her head, *I'm almost twice her age and not even… or, am I twice her age and twice engaged?*

"I know I'm young, Ma'am, and Robby is, too, but for both of us, there's something here inside that cannot be denied."

Mary Beth acknowledged Celeste's feelings with a smile that did not deter her from her purpose. "My best wishes, Celeste, but now I want you to think back a little. A great deal has happened recently, but really Austin was killed on Wednesday, only a few days ago. Can you remember where you were Wednesday after class?"

"Oh, yes, Ma'am. First I was just a rolling stone, wandering around a little. Then I remembered I was supposed to have dinner with Robby, so I was happy, like king of the road, at least king of Campus Lane. That's where I was. And even better, I met up with my two best friends and we…"

Mary Beth interrupted, "That's Liz and El."

"Yes, Ma'am, Liz and Ellie and I went to the student lounge for a coke and we had some snacks or something. Anyway, it was food, glorious food, and we just sat and talked and laughed for the longest time."

"Were you three together all afternoon?"

"No. I went on to the library. Maybe the others did, too. We remembered that you wanted us to write a critique on the article you wrote about Poe. If you'll excuse my saying so, that's hard to do, Ma'am. I'm not saying who, but some people are afraid to say they don't like it 'cause you might give them a lower grade. Not me, I liked it lots. It showed me that there are lots of different ways to look at a poem or a story and I shouldn't try so hard to be like the others."

"Thanks, Celeste. That's what I hoped students would gain from the reading, a little independent thinking. But as I said, what I want now is some information about what everyone was doing Wednesday afternoon, the afternoon that Austin Westlake was murdered. Don't worry, I'm not asking you for an alibi. This isn't official. I want to piece together a time sequence of who was where, when, and what that person might have seen. When you read a story by Poe or any other author, sometimes a minor detail is thrown into focus by the ending and changes the whole story. That's what I'm looking for, something you might have seen or heard."

"You mean you're like looking for a clue, Professor Mary Beth? Totally awesome. I've been waiting to say that. Liz says 'totally awesome' all the time and she's so cool. I'll really, really think on it, about it. You told us not to text you. I'll e-mail, unless it's really, really important and I really have to text."

"Liz and Robby can probably help more than I can. I mainly notice things that are different from Zambia. Like there are so many white people in Midfield. Everyone. And they all walk like cowboys in the movies. Not one lady I see could carry anything on her head. Liz and Robby will notice things that were different on Wednesday from the way they were earlier in the week and small details I don't even see…yet. I am learning."

"Can I ask you a question now?"

"Of course, Celeste. That's why we're here."

"Well, I didn't know because you're so rich and everything."

"Rich? Whatever gave you that idea?"

"You have a car. I've seen it. And I know you eat at restaurants some times. Not one of my professors in Lusaca had a car or ate in restaurants."

While Mary Beth voiced the typical American answer to that comment, "That's considered middle class here," she thought again of Celeste and how her outlook on life was so deeply influenced by the tragic Zambian national narrative. Celeste used the same words as other students did, "university, professor," but to her they meant something different.

Celeste, though, was thinking of something else, "What I wanted to ask you ma'am is, are you Christian?"

"Why no, Celeste, I'm not. I'm Jewish."

"Jewish? How fantastic. I've never met anyone Jewish. That means you'll live to be very old."

"I don't understand where you're coming from."

"Coming from? I'm right here."

"I'll explain later. Right now I don't know what you mean by saying I'll live a long time."

Mary Beth's question had pushed a button: "I've studied being Jewish with the missionaries who came to the village. The patriarch Abraham lived until he was 175 and his wife Sarah until she was 127. And Isaac was 180 years when he died and his wife Rebecca was 137. And…"

"That's enough. I understand. Those figures might not be exact and I'm not sure I'd like to live that long, but let's hope some of those longevity genes have been passed on. Thank you for telling me about it," Mary Beth added as an afterthought.

Convinced of Celeste's innocence, Mary Beth left her student and their ranging conversation for another day. She crossed campus, visibly shaking her head over Celeste, then nodding in agreement with herself and her plan to ask Liz and Ellie for office conferences. Her original plan, the one she made with Tony, to accidentally run into the students on campus, was going to be time consuming. She knew that the further in time one gets from the crime, the more difficult it becomes to solve. She had to follow all leads immediately.

As she walked and plotted, she took a few minutes to call Tony. He should be alerted to her change of tactics and to the fact that Celeste had no alibi at hand for late Wednesday afternoon. The call kept breaking up and Tony's voice was so distorted that she hung up mid-sentence. *He'll call back when he can distance himself from all of the machines in the shop,* she thought.

I need to speak with him. Too much is happening; classes and Tony I can handle. But a murder, a murder of a good friend at that, an attack on a colleague, and the huge complication of Gabe—all of that is making a confused jumble of my formerly simple life... I need to clear my mind with a good half-mile swim. If they'd let me drink wine and swim the thirty-six lengths at the same time, that would help even more.

CHAPTER TWENTY-TWO

"Some people go to priests; others to poetry; I to my friends."
—Virginia Woolf

In addition to the sense of proportion and brain cleansing gained from her swim, Mary Beth was helped to gain a better perspective by meeting her good friend Abby in the locker room. As close as they were, May Beth wasn't ready to tell Ab about Gabe. Her feelings were too strong, too frightening. They did talk about the two crimes. As always, Abby with her medical background, provided more insight.

"The autopsy is all sewn up, Mary Beth."

"Can you let me know what happened without any of your gruesome puns?"

"Well, preliminary results show that Austin is a tad overweight, but 100% healthy–outside of the fact that he's dead."

"Abby, stop it."

"Sorry. It's an occupational hazard. Laughter and tears are so close together. Most of us in the field prefer laughing."

"I'm with you, girl-friend, but can we get serious for a minute? What were you going to say about Austin?"

"Remember the tattoo you discovered, the one that wasn't a tattoo at all? It might be more eloquent than we thought. It was definitely made with one of the marking pens on his desk. And it was definitely made before death, probably while the poison was taking effect, while Austin could half-realize what was happening to him."

"Abby, I hear you telling me that the kind of rough circle above Austin's wrist is important. What could it mean? How did it get there? Did Austin draw it? Ohmigod, was he trying to tell us something that's taking us this long to figure out?"

"I'll know more about that eloquent tattoo and about Austin in a few days when we get the tox report. Meanwhile, I've had a number of meetings with Ted Guppy. I'm not a psychiatrist, but I have some post doc. training in the field as well as my medical degree and I am sure that Ted is not faking anything. Whether he was knocked over accidentally or purposefully I don't know. He's beginning to think it was accidental, that someone–he keeps saying the pizza man– someone wanted something from him and pushed him to get at it. He's not consistent in his story. He certainly doesn't deliver it in a linear or logical manner, but I think I can piece together most of what happened. Not who caused it to happen. You'll have to do that."

"Pizza does keep intruding into this story, doesn't it?"

"Write it up, Mary Beth. You're the lit person here. Call it the *Pizza pie Murders-Chicago style.*"

"OK, Ab, that is funny without being macabre. But what is it with these pizzas?"

"Seth thinks they mean something. He has Syl following the pizza trail."

"He could be doing that just to keep Syl from bungling more important matters in the case."

"True, but we are faced with a plethora of pizzas."

"Seth would say a passel of pizzas.

"Two pizzas do not a plethora or a passel make. How about a pack?"

"How about getting serious? How is Syl picking up the pizza trail? He doesn't have any pizza markers, does he?"

"No, nothing like that. Seth has him contacting every pizza shop in town asking about orders phoned in Wednesday. The twenty-third of September, the day of Austin's murder."

"I suppose it has to be done, but the two pizzas under suspicion could have been bought by any walk-in."

"Or could have been frozen pizzas popped into the microwave at home for a quick lunch and murder, speaking of which…?"

"Yes. Let's 'do' supper."

Giving her swimmer-friendly hair cut a quick shaping with the dryer, Mary Beth joined Abby, who was street ready. They headed for the nearest pizza shop.

Mary Beth knew herself well enough to understand that Friday evening's supper with Abby was probably a delaying tactic. She was reluctant to continue the line of questioning that could possibly prove that one of her students or a good friend was the culprit. I'm not doing that, she lectured herself. *That's the wrong way to look*

*at it. I'm not looking for guilt; I'm eliminating Liz, Celeste, Robby, El,
and even Professor Ted as suspects. Even if I'm unofficial. Even if it's
just for me. I'm clearing them.*

She was determined to make something more of sharing a pizza with Abby than time off from an unpleasant task. "Abby, you said
at the pool that it would take a few more days before you got the
toxicology report. Why does it take so long for it to get here? It
sure doesn't in murder mystery books or TV programs."

"Mary Beth, you have to understand that you and Austin are
not the only game in town. It's true that his is the only murder
right now in Midfield, but it's not the only murder the forensic
toxicologists have to deal with. We send our samples to Columbus,
to the Toxicology Associates at Ohio State's College of Medicine.
They have such a back-up. Analysts usually work on a number of
cases at the same time, and they're always behind schedule. One
reason is staff shortages; another is that toxicologists often spend
two days a week in court offering expert testimony."

Mary Beth cut in. "I appreciate the explanation, Ab. I know I
asked for it, but let's cut to the chase. Where does that leave us?"

"In not such a bad place. Austin's samples would normally have
to sit and wait. I think in this case, the Midfield murder is being
pushed to the head of the list because it's an on-going investigation." She smiled, "It doesn't hurt that our "down home" sheriff
knows everyone in Columbus."

Even without Abby's explanation, Mary Beth knew she would
have some waiting time. She determined to put her impatience to
practical use. For one thing, she had to make herself question the
other suspects, and sometime soon. Now she and Abby took a few
minutes to catch up with news about Abby's husband Amos and
his alpaca farm. Amos had occasionally taken courses at Midfield
Campus College, so Mary Beth had known him before Abby did.
Because his interests and career now centered on alpacas, he was
taking courses at the nearby agricultural college instead, enjoying them more than he had expected to. Mary Beth was reminded
again that finding Austin's killer wasn't everyone's top priority.

Her lonely feeling of being on her own in the search was somewhat mitigated by Abby's invitation, "Come to the next Mensa
meeting with me. A real girl detective will be the speaker."

"Ow, that hurts, Abby, but yes. I'll be glad to join you. Fun."

CHAPTER TWENTY-THREE

"There are some secrets which do not permit themselves to be told."
 —Edgar Allan Poe

That "I'm in this alone" feeling was re-enforced Saturday morning when Mary Beth got back to her office; even the computer seemed reluctant to work with her. She couldn't open "write mail," so she spent time deleting general messages from administration and various department chairs who consistently hit "everyone" when they sent out a message. She did not care when band practice was to be or if the Asian American Singing society needed volunteers to cook dinner for the next meeting.

Not wishing to be constantly interrupted in her work or private life, Mary Beth had told her own students to reach her by e-mail. Not by phone. Not by twitter. She could pace herself with the e-mail dings that she found less invasive than a barrage of tweets and rings. Now looking at her in-box, she saw that she would have to put in time later in the day to answer those student messages. Other return e-dresses caught her eye. Mary Beth smiled to herself. *I'll read Gabe's first.*

Then she would have time for the students. Many of the answers to their e-mails would turn into conversations she enjoyed. She was good at teaching her students to solve some of the problems they had made for themselves. This was one of the subjects she could discuss from experience. Sometimes those e-mail conversations led to material for a class lecture. That's how she had started to talk about writer's block. "I don't believe in it," Mary Beth told the first student who had asked for help with writer's anxiety. "Have you ever heard of bus driver's block? Sales clerk anxiety? Do bank tellers regularly get up and walk away in the middle of helping a client?"

A kinder, gentler Mary Beth discussed the subject in class, giving students specific exercises if they thought they were faced with it. "If you think you are suffering from writer's block, go over to the pool for a swim and think through a conversation your characters might be having as you complete your laps. A non-swimmer, but still stuck? Here's another suggestion: turn to a new page on your computer or legal pad and write a letter to a friend, a letter that you do not intend to mail, explaining your problem. You will have solved your problem by the time you finish your letter. You don't have any friends? Then play a mind game with yourself. Pick up a yellow legal pad and a pen. Try writing that way, computerless. You don't even have to continue the paragraph you were working on earlier. Write the end of your essay. Start a new one. Whether or not these exercises help, above all, keep writing," she told them.

Suddenly, her computer self-corrected; "write mail" opened. Mary Beth typed a quick note to Liz asking her to come to the office at the end of the afternoon. She decided to save Robby, Eleanor, and Ted until the next day—or two, if detecting on a personal level became too oppressive. She was determined to stay with the questioning technique. She knew that the accumulation and repetition of details would eventually have an effect on the investigation, possibly lead it in an unexpected direction.

For the present, Mary Beth returned to her academic work, proof reading an article she was going to submit to the *Publications of the Modern Language Association*, alternating that with correcting student papers to keep her mind fresh for both subjects.

She looked at her watch. It was within the half-hour, and there was Liz, bouncing in. *She really does have a bounce to her step and radiates joy when she moves*, Mary Beth thought. *I used to think 'bouncing in' was more of a metaphorical phrase than a real one. I'll suggest it to Celeste for her list.*

"Hi, Professor Mary Beth, what's up?" Liz asked while giving her jeans a quick yank down and her McCollege sweatshirt a reverse yank up to make sure her tramp stamp was showing. She then re-arranged herself for what she anticipated would be another comfortable conversation. This was Liz's attitude toward life in general, and for her, reality usually met expectations.

Mary Beth moved into her good cop routine. She quickly found that Liz's story of Wednesday afternoon's activities corresponded to Celeste's. Of course, that could mean that the girls had prepared an alibi together, but Mary Beth doubted that. Too many people would have seen or, in this case, not seen them at the student lounge and in the library.

Happy to be discussing time spent with her friends, Liz restrained herself from using the slight embellishments that would make her story more interesting and stayed with the facts. She said she had gone to the dorm for dinner about the time Celeste and Robby had gone out.

"Did you know they were engaged?" Mary Beth asked.

"Yes, Robby now wears African earrings he had made to match hers. That's a commitment alright, but I worry about the engagement. Celeste is a doll, a doll who knows nada about American men. Robby is like a nice guy and all that, and his dad is a prof, but I don't know if he is serious the way she is."

She paused and quickly continued. "Oh, I'm sure it will be fine. They both intend to finish school. They'll have plenty of time." Mary Beth could see that Liz was reassuring herself, not her English professor.

"Speaking of completing school, Liz, I've heard various rumors about what you want to do when you graduate. Do you have any plans, ambitions? Are you going to graduate school?"

Before Liz could answer, chemistry professor Ted Guppy wandered in, completely oblivious to the fact that he hadn't knocked and might be interrupting something. He beamed benignly at Liz, illuminating the room with his well-known smile that managed to say, "I don't know who you are and what does it matter? It's such a lovely day."

"Some of my leaves have been stolen, Mary Beth," he announced. "I would go into town to tell Seth if I could remember where his office is and how to get there without having to stop at the bar that's near it."

Mary Beth turned to Liz, "I'd like to finish this conversation tomorrow. Same time? Same place?" Coming from a professor and directed to a student, this was more command than request. Liz acquiesced.

As she moved around her small office, trying gracefully to usher Ted in and Liz out, Mary Beth managed to knock over a stack of books she had been meaning to put on student reserve at the library. Notes flew out as books hit floor, desk, chair. Everyone stopped. Unanimous unspoken agreement to ignore chaos was reached. Everyone started moving and speaking again. In mid-action Mary Beth continued to push Liz and pull Ted, while looking toward the disarray of books and papers and saying, "I'll get them later. Not important." One final push and she closed the door behind Liz.

"Now, Ted, take a seat. Would you like a cup of tea or coffee?"

"Yes," he said.

Not worth continuing. She brewed and poured some energizing black premium tea, using the process to pull herself from the reality of one interview to the reality or quasi-reality, seeing it was with Ted, of another.

Mary Beth feared that Ted could not enter her world. It was up to her to try to enter his. "Good to see you, Ted. What brings you here?"

"Mary Beth, are you the one with dementia?"

She blushed because he seemed aware of the way she had pigeon-holed him.

"What do you mean, Ted?"

"I just told you why I was here. I lost some leaves. Remember?"

"Oh, yes. Did you lose them from your yard?"

"Professor, look at me. I know I have problems, but stop patronizing me. I'm not yet at the state where I sit out in my yard counting the leaves as they fall from the trees. No, I lost them from my at-home lab."

"I don't understand."

"I felt well enough today to continue some experiments I was doing with materials obtained through unusual circumstances."

Mary Beth flashed back to seeing Ted pick up dried plant materials at Austin's gallery and surreptitiously (he thought) put them in his pockets. "Maybe you couldn't remember where Seth's office is because you didn't want to discuss this with him."

"It's a possibility, though not one germane to the problem," Ted said. He added, "I had coded different kinds of leaves with simple numerical values that included numbers one to six. I recognized the leaves at either end of the scale. Now numbers three and four, the ones I wanted to identify, are gone."

"Are these the ones you obtained through 'unusual circumstances'?

"Well, yes they are, Mary Beth. Since you have no official standing on the case, I don't mind telling you that what you suspect is true. I hesitate to use the word 'stole' or even 'borrowed.' Let's say, I picked up the two varieties from the floor of Austin's gallery. Most of the leaves on the floor were easily recognized herbs. One of the ones I picked up, I'm sure is marijuana; the other I did not recognize. I don't know how significant the marijuana is. Is it Austin's for his own use? Is he in business? A dealer? Or is it something he's keeping for someone else?

"That would explain the interest the four kids had in getting into the shop and looking around, wouldn't it? If they were looking for something that belonged to them...?"

"How long have the leaves been missing, Ted?"

"I'm beginning to remember. As I have to keep reminding you, I'm not at the stage of being able to hide my own Easter eggs. You were over at my house the day I was attacked, right?"

She nodded. "You have problems, Ted, but we can still trust your memory of that day."

"Did you notice any samples, any leaves on my desk that night?"

She nodded again.

"I think that's when it happened. I think the mustachioed pizza man took them."

Mary Beth, who had been half-consciously watching the "new mail" box with her peripheral vision, noticed that the latest ping had accompanied an e-mail from Gabe. She thought of the warmth she felt through her bones just looking at his e-dress. She thought of being in his arms, such good arms. She thought she had better pay attention to Ted and his mad mustachioed pizza man.

"Ted, thanks for telling me about this. I'll discuss it with Sheriff Seth and get back to you. The leaves have to be a link between the two crimes, Austin's murder and your being roughed up."

Before Ted had closed the door behind him, Mary Beth had hit "read." She blushed as she read what Gabe said in his brief e-mail, "I like my body when it is with your body. Love."

She felt a Wow! go through her. *If I were writing an e-epistolary novel like Liz is not, I would have this be the first e-mail in the story. But, this isn't fiction, Mary Beth. This is real life, Girl. Your real life.* "I'll think about it tomorrow," she said out loud. "I'll just bask in it now."

CHAPTER TWENTY-FOUR

"I used to smoke marijuana. But I'll tell you something: I would only smoke it in the late evening. Oh, occasionally the early evening, but usually the late evening—or the mid-evening. Just the early evening, mid-evening and late evening. Occasionally, early afternoon, early mid-afternoon, or perhaps the late-mid-afternoon. Oh, sometimes the early-mid-late-early morning... But never at dusk."

—Steve Martin, writer, actor, comedian

Sunday was a game changer. Abby's news almost eclipsed any information Mary Beth had gained from her interview with Ted. After a quick call to make sure Mary Beth was in her office, Abby stopped by. "The FAX came into the office late last night. I wanted to deliver the news in person.

"We've got it," she said waving a sheaf of documents in Mary Beth's face. "I told you the Midfield Murder might get pushed to the top of the list."

"Abby, what 'list'? What have we 'got'?"

"The tox lab and the poison. It's belladonna."

"That's a plant, deadly nightshade, isn't it?"

Abby answered with a flurry of disjointed sentences: "Yes. And, Mary Beth, remember the scratches and dents you saw on Austin's desk? Those were fresh. We should have recognized them for what they were. Signs of convulsive kicking. That's a symptom of belladonna poisoning. More later. I have to be at work. Now. In fact, ten minutes ago. We'll talk, this afternoon probably. Keep the printouts. Seth said I could give them to you—or anyone actually. Read them later. They go into interesting details and not so interesting jargon."

Abby was gone with Mary Beth's perplexed appreciation hanging in the air, and Mary Beth herself reaching for books, brief case, papers, and thoughts of what she was going to be doing and saying during the next few days of teaching. In the light of such interesting news of a real crime, it was hard to keep Poe's fictive mysteries uppermost in her mind, but during class preparation, she became so involved with his arm chair Detective August Dupin that she forgot about her own detecting work for much of the day.

Later in the afternoon she met with Robby, suspect #5 on Tony's list. Over a coke for him and a cup of green tea for her, the interview started with an abrupt question from Robby, "What's the agenda, professor? Why do you want to talk with me?"

"I want to ask you some questions about where you were on Wednesday afternoon."

"Last Wednesday?" he asked, somewhat perplexed.

"No, Robby, I'm talking about September 23."

"It figures," he said, pulling slightly on his ear, which made Mary Beth notice that he was wearing the new earrings, the small African hoops that Liz had told her about. *This must be as much of a public announcement as they are going to make*, she thought, but decided to stay on subject. She listened as Robby explained.

"Celeste told me that's what you wanted with her. And Liz told me that's what you wanted with her. That would make Ellie next. It's all about Austin, not school work. Good. I also heard you discovered the body, professor."

"How did you hear that?" she asked trying to keep suspicious and accusing tones out of her voice.

"The grapevine climbs quickly at McCollege," he answered.

"I did discover the body, Robby. It was a terrible shock for me. Discovering a body would be, but discovering the body of a close friend was, was—I still can't believe it. Better not to think about it. I'm certainly not going to talk about it now."

"Professor, Austin was a close friend of mine, too. He really put himself out for me the way no one else would. I wish he was still with us."

"Were still with us," Mary Beth started to say. She stopped herself. Robby wouldn't tell her anything if he thought she was going to correct his grammar every time he opened his mouth.

"How did you come to be such good friends, Robby?"

"Well, I'm interested in the stuff he collects. He knows a lot about a lot of different things. And he offered to store some things for me. As a friend. Not on consignment or anything."

Mary Beth's internal alert buttons went off. *Careful now. I don't know how it happened, but this conversation is taking part on multiple levels.*

"Was Austin storing art objects for you, Robby? Or some collection you have?"

"Not exactly." Robby thought for a moment. "You're going to find out anyway. I know Professor Guppy is analyzing some materials he found in Austin's shop. He talks about it in class. We all laugh at him because he forgets things like where the class meets, but he sure knows his chemistry. He's one of my best teachers. Oh, excuse me, professor. You are in your own way, too."

"Forget it, Robby. Step back a minute. What am I going to find out anyway and what does it have to do with what Austin was storing for you?"

"Well, I couldn't store stuff at home because I wouldn't want to get my dad in trouble. He's up for tenure now and has enough problems with people who don't like him, and maybe it's true that he hasn't made a national name for himself, but hey, this is McCollege, how many profs have made a name for themselves. Present company excluded, I'm sure. Excuse me again. Everyone knows your books are required reading, and not only in your own classes." He smiled.

Pleased, she tried not to show it. "Forget it, again, Robby. Where are you wandering off to? I know your dad has problems. That's not what we're talking about."

"In our house, that's what we're always talking about."

"Robby."

"Yes, ma'am. Well, Austin was keeping my stash of marijuana for me. He kept some in the glass jars that had all the other leaves in them. You know, like in Poe's 'The Purloined letter,' he kept the clue in the obvious place and no one noticed. I really like how well plotted Poe's short stories are. I'm trying to do that with my life."

Mary Beth didn't want to interrupt, but felt that Robby's attempt to impress his teacher was getting him off subject. She didn't have to say anything as Robby stopped for a few tortuous minutes, grappling with something. He used the time to hem and haw, or the student equivalent. After a few 'wells' and 'ya'knows,' he added, "Well, there is, ya'know, more stored in other places."

"Robby, I don't care. Well, rather I do care, but it's not something I want to discuss now. Later. I need to think. As a friend of your parents this information puts me in a bind. It's a problem, but not in the same league as finding Austin's murderer. Thank you for telling me, for trusting me. If I'd known anything like this was coming, I wouldn't have made another appointment for right now."

"Are you saying you want me to leave?"

She stood up.

He left.

CHAPTER TWENTY-FIVE

"Cupid is a knavish lad."
 —William Shakespeare, *A Midsummer Night's Dream*

Mary Beth's other Sunday appointment wasn't part of her academic or detecting lives. It was a dinner at Luigi's in Akron with Gabe. Akron isn't exactly a half-way point between Midfield and Cleveland, but it's close enough so that both Mary Beth and Gabe felt they were giving a little of their independence and gaining a little commitment.

Gabe was already seated at one of the wooden booths when Mary Beth arrived. They grasped hands across the table, then, half-embarrassed, studied the plastic menus that were already on the table, not that anyone has ever ordered anything but spaghetti at Luigi's. Gabe looked up from the menu. Mary Beth was gesticulating with her face, making her features into an overall "shh, shhh" signal and, not as discreetly as she thought, pointing her eyes first to the left, then to the right. She then became preoccupied with the menu, holding it up to her eyes and reading it carefully; that is, she would have been reading it carefully if she weren't holding it upside down. Gabe, understanding from her unsubtle sign language that he wasn't to talk, tried to turn his face into a big question mark. Mary Beth's reply was to conceal herself deeper in the "today's side dishes" column of the menu. Everyone else in the restaurant was oblivious to the mimed mini-drama being played out at booth 22.

After a few more minutes of Mary Beth and Gabe's intense quiet, the couple at the table next to them paid their bill and left.

As soon as they were gone, Mary Beth began to speak in a subdued voice, "Thanks, Gabe. I appreciate your being quiet for a few minutes while I picked up their conversation."

"Whose conversation? What's going on?"

"You haven't been part of my life long enough to know this, but one of my more obscure talents is being able to listen to a conversation at a nearby table while carrying on an animated conversation of my own. I do it automatically; it doesn't mean anything. But this time I could hear the couple talking about a college student who they felt had gotten in with the wrong crowd. I stopped talking so I could hear even better. Robby must have been the topic of the conversation, though they didn't mention any names."

"Then why does it have to be your friend Robby?"

"Well, they said his dad is a Midfield prof, which limits it somewhat. They also said that he hangs out with a bunch of girls who are up to no good."

"Mary Beth, that means nothing, zilch. You have no idea who those strangers were talking about and even if it turns out to be Robby, you have no idea what their standards of good and no good are."

"Gabe, what? Are you trying to tell me that I'm supposing too odd of a coincidence? You're still a newcomer. You'll find out soon enough that in this part of Ohio, everyone knows everyone else and more, is probably related. To me, the conversation means I'm following the right track." Even in her anxiety, Mary Beth took time to say "I'm following" not "Tony and I are following."

"Hearing, OK, overhearing," she corrected herself in response to a look on his face. "Yes, overhearing something like that makes me realize that I'm doing the smart thing in interviewing my four students. It strengthens my motivation. I've been too casual. I'm going to be more meticulous in my questioning as I continue to meet with the students, and continue I will."

She was overcome with guilt. This was a conversation she should be having with Tony and now she was having it with Gabe. *I'll call Tony tomorrow morning. Maybe he'll come over for breakfast. What we've had together is something very special.* She paused, *What I have with Gabe is more. I know that. And that's the problem.*

As if reading her mind, Gabe reached over and put his hand over hers, instilling her with confidence and with a warmth she had not known before.

"Mary Beth," he said, "I'm sure you will be successful in identifying the criminal mind-set of your students, if there is one, but what about other successes in your life. It's time to move out of your comfort zone."

CHAPTER TWENTY-SIX

"Belladonna. Noun,
In Italian, A beautiful lady. In English. A deadly poison.
Striking example of the essential identity of the two tongues."
    —Ambrose Bierce

Mary Beth tried not to think about what Gabe was asking her to risk when Tony stopped by early Monday morning. The two amateur detectives shared a quick planning meal of sour dough English muffins with Frank Cooper's Vintage Marmalade. They decided to pour tea into one thermos, coffee into another, and stop at the donut shop for a dozen mixed, plain, and chocolate covered on their way to an unannounced visit to Seth's office. They offered first donut choice to the Sheriff Department's receptionist, at work early, and went into Seth's office.

"Donuts for a policeman? Pretty stereotypical. But I'll take them anyway. Thanks," was Seth's response to the offered gift.

Tony started the conversation, not rudely but without the niceties that Mary Beth would have introduced, "We're here to find out something about the poison, Seth."

"Well, I didn't think this was a social call. I'm glad to tell you what I can. I'm not giving you any privileged information, Tony, or you either, Mary Beth. *The Daily Record* has already carried the belladonna news. Anyone who is interested can look it up. I do have the advantage of the tox lab's sending me information that might not be readily available on the internet."

Mary Beth leaned forward and used her fingers to comb back the hair that was falling in her eyes. "Seth, we really appreciate your giving us data from Internet membership-only files."

"Mary Beth, I'm not sure if this comes under Ohio's Open Records and Open Meetings laws, what you probably call the Sunshine Laws, but if giving you access to the lab report on belladonna will help you to find Austin's murderer, let it be.

"First and most important and, as we unfortunately have seen, belladonna is fatal if eaten. Just about any part of it is fatal, plus you wouldn't notice by sight or smell if it had been used as a food additive. But, some things are noticeable even to the amateur. For example, the berries are notoriously sweet, so your friendly neighborhood poisoner would put them in a fruit pie, not a pizza. The seeds, which weren't used in this case, are small, like you'd see in a fig.

"What did poison Austin were the dried leaves. They'd have a slightly bitter taste, but no odor, so you could partially crush them, add a little sugar and oregano, which, F.Y.I., is what our killer did, sprinkle them over a slice of pizza, and the victim would never have noticed, especially since the poison is highly active. It wouldn't take much."

"I'm sure Austin was trying to tell us that as best he could," Mary Beth interjected. The tattoo-that-wasn't had to have been his attempt to draw a pizza on the only surface he had available, his arm."

Tony continued Mary Beth's line of thought, "You're right, Mary Best. I'll bet that line from the center to the circumference was his attempt to show a slice of the pizza. He was trying to leave a meaningful clue."

"That must have been after he ate it," Seth added to the excited roll. "I've been reading about poisonous plants. Belladonna is easily identifiable. If you look under a microscope, you'll see that the leaves have minute white prominences, but c'mon, what pizza eater stops scarfing long enough to microscopically examine what he's eaten? Not Austin. Not anyone."

Mary Beth had stopped taking notes at this exchange. She asked, "So what happens when you eat the stuff, Seth? Do you just up and die?"

Seth took a look at his own notes, "The active agent that the plant contains is atropine—let me read this part to you–'The atropine disrupts the parasympathetic nervous system's ability to regulate non-volitional, subconscious activities such as sweating, breathing, and heart rate.'"

"Breathing and heart rate. There you are. With all of those big words how simple and how dreadful."

"It's dreadful all right, Mary Beth, but it's not as simple as it used to be. Our toxicology labs and scientists are pretty savvy when it comes to poisons, so these days, homicidal poisonings are rare. I've got here the results of a 2009 study from another college, the University of Georgia. The study checks on the federal mortality rate between 1998 and 2005. It found 523 poison murders in the U.S. during that period. That's less than 1% of all homicides. People think there's been a slight uptick in the past five years. Even if there has been, poison is still responsible for only a small percentage of all murders."

Mary Beth leaned forward again, "Is it possible it was an accident, Seth? Is it possible that someone wanted to put Austin out of commission for a short time and the drug, the belladonna, was stronger than expected?"

"No, Mary Beth."

"I know I'm reaching. It's just so impossibly sad to think of what Austin was: someone's son, a brother, friend, probably a lover, a respected member of Midfield's business and arts complex. Now it's all gone because of someone's perceived need of what? Something Austin had?"

Becoming more emotional as she talked and more distracted from the reality of being in Seth's small office, Mary Beth's natural clumsiness took over. With one emphatic sweep of her arm, Seth's book and papers went flying.

The meeting was over.

CHAPTER TWENTY-SEVEN

"Within the mind of a killer, complex feelings are eerily simple. This is why killers can shoot men in Reno just to watch them die, and the rest of us usually can't."
  —Chuck Klosterman, *Sex, Drugs, and Cocoa Puffs: A Low Culture Manifesto*

As Mary Beth, slightly chagrined, and Tony, too intent to notice, walked back to their respective work stations, Tony challenged their investigative technique. "I think we're going about it the wrong way."

Immediately wary, Mary Beth asked, "What do you mean?"

"What do you mean, what do I mean? I mean, if we're trying to find Austin's murderer, we're kicking the can in the wrong direction."

With a semblance of cool, Mary Beth answered, "I still don't know what you mean, Tony. We're not real detectives, you know. We each have a day job and various relationships to consider." She blushed. Strangely, so did he.

"Instead of thinking of how to solve this crime, why don't we put our feet in the murderer's shoes? Why don't we think how we would commit the crime and, more important, why we, the murderer, think we have to do away with Austin and hit poor Guppy over the head?"

"He didn't hit Guppy. Guppy fell, or so the word is on campus."

"Whatever."

"You're right. Y'know, Poe talked about that too. He uses nineteenth century language, but it translates to the same thing. He says to solve a puzzle you need 'an identification of the reasoner's intellect with that of his opponent.' It's not that easy for me. Before I put my feet in the murderer's shoes, I have to visualize him or her. I have to have a name for the murderer. I can't start claiming him without naming him."

"Well, Mary Beth, giving her or him a name doesn't mean that we'll understand motivations and other stuff. After all, the tongue is just another muscle. But if you think it will help, I'll agree. How about, 'The Pizza Delivery-man'? Between the lab report and Austin's poorly drawn but eloquent clue, we know that's whodunit."

"Let's shorten it to 'The Pizza-man.' Never use three words when two will do. That's straight from my Freshman Comp class."

"Do we know it's a man?"

"Doesn't the moustache disguise point to a male culprit?"

"It would except that it's Guppy who identifies him or her or it."

"Let's go with the pizza man. We can always revise later. That's from Freshman Comp, too."

"What I see is that this pizza-man guy can move freely around campus, but he likes to complicate things."

"I wonder why. For right now, let's say he's just one person, not a conglomerate. He seems to have walked into Austin's apartment with no problem. Nothing was disturbed; the door was partly opened—for him?

"But when he went to see Ted Guppy who was not to be killed and who potentially could be an identifying witness, he wore a fake Italian moustache that complicated the issue. I think our unknown perp, the pizza man, has a good sense of humour."

"I like the way we're reconstructing the character of this guy, Tony. Let me add, I don't see him as a professional killer. He might not have ever murdered anyone before, which doesn't mean that he won't do it again if he gets away with this one. And he won't. We won't let him. Where was I?"

"On a descriptive roll, Mary Beth. Go on."

"He's not a hands-on murderer, not a shooter or a choker. He's a murderer who wants to distance himself from the crime. That would be a reason for using a poison, something that acts later."

"You're right, Mary Beth. He made sure he wasn't there when Austin actually died. For all we know, before he left, he sat with Austin for a half-hour, convivially eating pizza, making sure he was working on the non-poisoned half!"

Mary Beth raced ahead with the idea, "He might have spent that imaginary half an hour telling jokes, flattering Austin into being relaxed with him. He might have even tried to negotiate a price or a trade for whatever it is that Austin had and he wanted. Is there an antidote for belladonna? Maybe he would have applied it if he had gotten the–the what? There's the rub. What did he want?"

"Whoa, Mary Beth I think you're going too far abroad."

"You're mixing metaphors, Tony."

"Stop it, Teach. Do you know you've almost proven that the pizza man is a nice guy?"

"Maybe we should say pizza person, Tony. It's beginning to sound more and more like a woman. And poison is usually considered a woman's weapon."

"Anyway, Mary Beth, whether it's murder that's intimate or murder at a distance, it's still murder. Austin is dead."

"Thanks for keeping me on target, Tony. I think the pizza man, or now, woman, is young. The perp doesn't have to be a student, but young enough so that no one would notice, she hesitated, 'it' on campus."

"Mary Beth, the murder didn't take place on campus."

"My bad. Mixed metaphor or not, you were right to say whoa, Tony. I am going too far abroad. I know Austin was killed in his apartment. I'm the one who found him. I'm such an amateur in this detecting business. I can't even keep my facts in order."

"Hey, Mary Best, don't put us amateurs down. Remember amateurs built the Ark; professionals built the Titanic. So, let's take a breath here and get some distance. Go back to the concept of using poison for an impersonal murder, what you called murder at a distance. Do we have someone who didn't want to dirty her hands? Someone with a little misplaced maturity?"

Tony looked up at the street crossing. "Right now, hon, I don't know about the murder or anything. I can't tell you how happy I am to turn off here and go on to the shop and work on real things: wheels and brakes and gears and handlebars. Talk with you later today, Mary Best."

CHAPTER TWENTY-EIGHT

"I have great faith in fools—my friends call it self-confidence."
—Edgar Allan Poe

As Mary Beth and Tony headed in different directions, Tony temporarily freed from thoughts of murder, Mary Beth so deeply steeped in them that she didn't see Eleanor, dressed for battle, came running up to her. She mentally returned to the present and to El.

That girl! She's always dressed for confrontation. I've never seen her without her black tee and those Doc Martens that look like they've used up their life-time guarantee. Then Mary Beth remembered something else. She was supposed to meet Eleanor for coffee. She looked at her watch. Now.

She made a quick recovery, "Hi, Eleanor, I don't know how this worked out, almost in the middle of the street, but you're right on time for our appointment. I'll buy you something to drink. Where would you like to go?"

"Let's go to Tea-total. Liz and me think it's better than Starbucks."

Mary Beth swallowed her reprimand. As they sat on the small booth's scuffed plastic seats, she studied the beautiful student sitting opposite her with a degree of wariness. Today's black tee sported a McCollege logo with a jagged red nail polish line drawn through it. *What's that all about?* Mary Beth realized that she knew less about El than she did about the other three members of the fearsome four, or whatever the group was self-named. She wondered, *Could El be the perp? What in the world could Austin used to have that she wanted?*

The student server brought their order, green tea (Mary Beth) and chocolate tea (El) plus fresh croissants. With her hands splayed at the edge of the table, Mary Beth leaned forward ready for verbal action.

Eleanor beat her to it. "Those smell heavenly, Professor. Thanks loads, but, they won't help you with my year-end faculty evaluation 'cause I'm getting out of here."

Taken aback, Mary Beth reminded herself why she was meeting El and who El was. El, from Hell, is right, she told herself and regained control.

"Eleanor, we'll skip the abruptness of your remark and the insinuation that I would 'buy' a student's approval with a croissant. You're insulting yourself more than you're insulting me. Think about it. What interests me is your saying that you plan to leave. Do you mean leave Midfield College Campus or only the English Department?"

"Mary Beth, I would've, could've, should've left here at the beginning of the semester, but I thought I'd give it one more try. I do like my friends, though they're getting odder. I like some courses, yours, for instance, and that special chem. course McCollege is famous for, though sometimes I wonder where Professor Guppy is leading us, or if he even knows. That's what happens when you inhale all those chemicals," she muttered.

"Then why are you leaving? You must know that you're a 'person of interest' in Austin's murder case as well as in the roughing up of Professor Guppy."

"C'mon, no one is seriously thinking of me as a possible murderer. You know that. And to get to your first question without offending you twice in one coffee break, the atmosphere around here isn't exactly what you'd call intellectually stimulating."

Mary Beth's eyes went to the jagged line across the college logo. *There was an easy explanation for it, after all.*

El was still explaining, "I visited a friend at the University of Chicago a week or so ago. The lab there was such an exciting place. I gave them some of Professor Guppy's samples, you know, the ones he lifted from Austin, the ones Austin kept in his collectible bottles on the shelf."

"What, Eleanor? How did you know? How did you get the samples? What happened to them? Did you take them from Dr. Guppy's office when he was knocked out?" For a minute Mary Beth thought she had a new and real clue. Eleanor dashed that thought.

"No big deal. Guppy gave me some crumbles to play with. When I brought them to Chicago, right away, the guys in the lab separated the marijuana from the combination of oregano and belladonna. They said that the oregano was probably used to disguise the belladonna. Here no one at the college cares."

Except whoever it was who stole the rest of the "crumbles" that Ted Guppy had collected, Mary Beth thought and for once didn't correct her thoughts before she said, "I care." She wanted to keep on topic, but wondered silently if the use of the diminutive word "crumbles" was a tool to make the potential crimes of stealing unimportant.

Foremost was staying on topic, catching up with the conversation. At first she pictured the havoc El would wreak at the U. of C. *Maybe not. They'd seen her kind before.* Then the importance of what Eleanor had implied seeped in: *the belladonna had been in plain view on Austin's shelf.* Mary Beth was startled at receiving such important information about the poison from such an unexpected source. Her thoughts turned to class, *In plain sight, just like the missing letter in Poe's "The Purloined Letter." I can see Austin planning to store the marijuana that way, sort of a visual pun. Little did he know how his "trick" would be used.*

"I know you care, Mary Beth. I know you and Austin were close friends. And my own close friends have told me that you're interrogating every one you can get your hands on. Excuse me saying so, I probably wouldn't, but since I'm leaving Midfield anyway, here goes: it doesn't seem a logical crime-solving technique to me."

"I'll find some logic in it," Mary Beth retorted. "I've helped Sheriff Seth solve crimes around here before."

She had to leave. It wasn't until later that she realized she had not followed up on El's strange comment about the fearsome four becoming "odder."

"I'm having a hard time balancing all the balls that make up my life," Mary Beth told Tony that night. She did not include that very special balancing act needed to keep from showing the euphoria or despondency that took control every time she heard or did not hear from Gabe. She also did not include the overwhelming guilt she was beginning to feel every time she was with Tony. *I've always been a one-man woman,* she thought. *Almost always,* she corrected, remembering the writers conference she had attended last year.

"Yes, I'm having a hard time," she said bringing the conversation and her thoughts back to the present.

"I learned so much from El," she reported, "but I can't take this one-on-one investigating much longer. Eleanor didn't squirm a bit. I did. The more she talked, the queasier I felt. I don't want one of my students to be a murderer. I've had enough."

"We can't quit now, Mary Babe. All you have to do is to finish your interview with Robby. You were interrupted first time around. He'll be your last interviewee."

"Tony, I have a better idea. I'm so tired of talking to these good kids about bad things. Instead let's invite Robby and his parents for Saturday brunch. It will be more relaxed than a one-on-one interview and it won't be any work for me. I won't cook. Bagels and smoked salmon should cover it."

"That's not thorough enough, Mary Babe. It's like we're giving Robby clear sailing, plus putting off our investigation almost another week."

"I know, but, as I keep saying, we do have day jobs. As far as Robby goes, we'll need a follow up, another one-on-one. But I think if the five of us sit around and talk informally, the two of us, that's you and I, will find some good leads to follow with Robby. Plus I've been meaning to have the Sayers over for ages; Peggy's always been so kind to me."

She added, "We'll have to be careful, though. I have no idea if Peggy and George know of their son's pot habit, and I sure don't want to be the one to tell them"

"Me either, Mary Beth. Something else, Hon, I know this isn't the time and place, but you and I should have a one-on-one ourselves."

"What are you saying, Tony?"

"I'm saying that I'm getting different vibes from you."

"And I from you, for that matter."

"That's it, Mary Beth. It's not that we don't see each other, don't talk. We talk all the time about Austin and who killed him." Tony held a hand up to stop the interruption he knew was coming. "I know that's important—to both of us. After that, our conversation kind of deteriorates to whether you should have padding on your handlebars or not."

"I understand, Tony. And I agree. We'll talk later. Now should we invite the three Sayers over?"

"I'm good, Mary Beth. We've nothing to lose. Probably nothing to gain either, except a good time with Peggy and George. You don't have to worry. I won't spill the beans or whatever it is that Robby is grinding up and smoking."

CHAPTER TWENTY-NINE

"Economists report that a college education adds many thousands of dollars to a man's lifetime income—which he then spends sending his son to college."
—Bill Vaughn, 1971

The casual invitation went out and was accepted in the same spirit. Professor and Mrs. Sayers, proud parents of Robby, and Robby himself arrived on time, hungry, and all wearing just-out-of-the-dryer jeans, showing Peggy's strong influence. More of that influence was visible with each member of the family carrying a small hostess gift: a cleverly arranged collection of stones found in their latest hike in the Charm River bed, a purple hyacinth plant that perfumed the room, and from Robby an old, though more ratty than valuable, edition of E.A. Poe's poems.

Tony mixed Mimosas while everyone relaxed. He knew that it wasn't the alcohol content, but rather the ritual of popping the champagne cork, mixing it with fresh orange juice, and adding that final touch of a liqueur marinated strawberry that covered the first few minutes of awkwardness that even old friends can feel as they move from one environment to another.

After Peggy and George admired Mary Beth's natural looking centerpiece (hurriedly assembled from some branches recently fallen from trees, it was more natural that they knew), all dipped into the pre-brunch hummus, and the conversation veered, as it usually did, to academic politics.

George didn't observe any of the niceties. He didn't ask about class registration or size. He didn't ask Mary Beth if she had published any articles lately or if she was going to the M.L.A. Conference this year.

He leaped right in with criticism: "How are you getting along with the English Department old fogies? Lost in the obscurities of Feminist Critical Thinking, still deriding Derrida, aren't they?" he asked. "You'll excuse me, but what we really say in the History Department every time your friend Hake stand up at a faculty meeting is, "There he goes, f'ing with Foucault again.'"

Mary Beth smiled at the alliterations and struggled to come up with an answer that would not cast more aspersions on her colleagues. The English Department had its problems, but some of its members were good friends and did not hide behind a curtain of trendy, politically correct quotations no one could understand.

George didn't wait for her answer. His interest was really not in the English Department and any problems Mary Beth might think she had. "You don't have the problems that I have though. You guys provide a service to the College with all of your writing courses. The History Department is becoming extinct and they want to cut their losses. Me. What I need is to publish one definitive article, not an evaluation of research, not a review of a book, but an article about something I and only I have access to. Then they'll want me, tenure me, adore me." He laughed, "They sure don't now."

Mary Beth could see that Robby was embarrassed by the nakedness and bitterness of his father's disclosure. She changed the subject, keeping it away from what she surmised would be another sensitive area, the rumors of Robby's engagement to Celeste. Did his parents know?

"Robby, have you given any thought to what field you'll go into after graduation?"

"Not academics. That's for sure," he replied. "I'm taking the LSATs and I'll probably go on to law school. I'm pretty interested in intellectual property. Like all that literary stuff Austin collected as a side-line." This introduction of Austin's name into ordinary conversation gave Mary Beth a pang that she was not expecting. Tony could see she was affected and moved to be next to her.

They listened half-heartedly as Robby explained his interest in intellectual property. "If you're a painter and you sell your painting, then it belongs to the person you sold it to. But if you write some letters, who do they belong to? The person you wrote to? The writer? The person who finds them in an old box? The person who buys them from the finder? The writer's estate? It goes on and on," Tony became involved in the Robby's monologue and interrupted, "Gee, e-mail must have caused a tsunami change in that field. Think of all the writers and politicians for starters who write and don't hit 'save.'"

The oven gave a ring that closed the subject and reminded Mary

Beth she was cook as well as hostess. The bagels were toasted. As they filled their plates, everyone was very polite about Mary Beth's typical foray into imported (from New York) smoked salmon. This time it was pastrami flavored. Not bad was the consensus. "Why does she continue to experiment?" was the unasked question.

The small party became more relaxed as the afternoon wore on and the pitcher of Mimosas was refilled. Tenure problems were temporarily forgotten and campus gossip took their place. George couldn't wait to be the first to pass on the news.

"Did you hear that Hake sprained his ankle. He's telling everyone it's your fault, Mary Beth."

"My fault? What in the world do you mean? I didn't know about it until this minute."

"He says he was rushing to get some papers you needed and twisted his ankle running down the stairs."

"My fault that he's getting some papers he wants to give me, so I'll do some work for him? Oh, it's not worth confronting him. I hope he can make classes tomorrow, though. Otherwise I'm going to end up getting the blame plus the extra assignment of covering his class for him."

Tiring of faculty news, Robby became almost eloquent about himself, while managing to skirt the subject of Celeste. "I'll accept family advice," he said when he got on the subject of graduate school. "But after that, I'm not listening to anyone, If Henry Ford had listened to the suggestions he got, instead of a car, he would have made a faster horse. That's all that people wanted."

Mary Beth laughed and said, "What I want, Robby, is your help. Let's meet at Ye Olde Gaol's bar at 4 o'clock Monday."

Robby recognized a command when he heard one and nodded agreement.

Mary Beth and Tony agreed that a pleasant time was had by all. "It was fun, Tony. But now I'm so tired I can't think. It seems to me a lot was going on. At times I wanted to nudge you, but how could I in front of our guests? I was sure that some things that were said possibly pertained to the murder. Was it some remark of George's? Or maybe it was Robbie, or that sweet Peggy? Some words seemed odd at the time. Let's hope I remember tomorrow." Whatever it was she had heard, something she wanted to remember to repeat to Tony, now eluded her.

One thing Mary Beth did remember was hearing George say to Peggy after their profuse thanks at the door, "Some things, smoked salmon for one, are best left alone."

CHAPTER THIRTY

"There is no evidence that the tongue is connected to the brain."
—Frank Tygen

Robby arrived at Ye Olde Gaol promptly at four o'clock on Monday afternoon, just as Mary Beth was tucking herself into one of the high backed, wooden booths.

"This place is really creepy in the afternoon," Robby said. "Did you notice we're the only ones here?"

"Did you notice we're in Midfield?" was her retort. "It does make for a private conversation," she added.

"Speaking of privacy," Robby said, "I want to thank you for not bringing up my pot smoking in front of my parents yesterday. I've made up my mind to talk with them about it tonight. I don't think they'll care too much. I'm not a dealer or anything. But I do think they'd care if they heard it from someone else first. Not from me."

By then, Mary Beth was sipping her Australian Shiraz and Robby his caffeinated diet coke. Wanting to show approval, Mary Beth put her wine glass down and reached across the table to give Robby an encouraging slap on the back. Neither she nor the table was made for such a maneuver. Her arm hit Robby's. Robby splashed his coke on his favorite Bolivian sweater, a striped Evo Morales that presumably announced his idealized politics. Unfortunately, it was one of those symbols that went unrecognized by most of his classmates. In the confusion, he choked on what he was trying to swallow, and in a voice a few registers down from his own, strangled out "I'm OK. I'll be OK."

Mary Beth realized that any action she'd take would only make the situation worse. As she prepared to wait through a few minutes of coughing, she heard the unmistakable voice of Dr. Theodore Guppy singing, "I hear the pizza man. Yes, I hear the pizza man."

She leaned around the side of the scratched and stained wooden back to face the bar where Guppy was doing his well-known dance, the one he did when a student in class finally understood what he had been saying or when a brighter one broke new ground. Mary

Beth had heard of the Guppy jig, but had never seen it. As far as she knew, this was the first out-of-class performance.

Still twisted in her booth, she applauded, but then stopped with her right hand mid-way to meeting her left. She realized what the victory dance meant.

Guppy half-strutted, half soft-shoed his way toward the booth. Robby looked frightened. He had stopped coughing and was trying to pick up his paper napkin from the floor.

"Robby," she said, "sit up. In fact, stand up for your professor. You can't try to hide now."

Although Mary Beth and Robby were well aware of the implications of Guppy's discovery, he was not. He took the seat Robby offered and repeated, "I heard the pizza man. Yes, I heard the pizza man." Then it dawned on him. Counting the bartender, only four people were in Ye Olde Gaol's bar. He eliminated himself. If he had heard the voice of the pizza delivery man, it had to be one of the other people there. He knew it wasn't the bartender. He had been talking with him. Guppy looked more bewildered than usual.

Mary Beth said, "We have to talk this out."

Robby looked as if he would cry. He did cry in long hysterical sobs. Guppy looked more bewildered. He put his hand on Robby's shoulder to comfort him. Robby tried to shrug it away. "I don't deserve..." That's as far as he got before being racked with sobs again.

Left elbow on table, Mary Beth rubbed her face with her right hand and pushed her hair back from her forehead. She finally removed her hand from where it had come to rest covering her mouth in denial. "This is not one hundred percent clear to me, Robby. And it's not at all clear to Professor Guppy. You had better tell us what you know, what you did in reference to Guppy and the samples he took from Austin's."

Ted Guppy interrupted, "I think I do know what happened, but I want the whole story, young man. And I want it in your words. If no harm was intended, which I'm sure was the case, I promise you right now I will not prosecute. Your story will not leave this room." He looked around, "this bar."

Guppy's generosity brought more tears from Robby.

"Robby," Mary Beth said sharply. "I know you're upset, but you're letting yourself get hysterical. Or are you using those tears to stall while you make-up another alibi? It won't do you any good.

You are the pizza-man. A few minutes ago when you were choking and your voice dropped a few registers, Professor Guppy recognized it. It was the same as the disguised voice you adopted when you came to his house."

Mary Beth willed herself to be silent. She had already said more than she should. She made herself wait to see if Robby would do what so many others do, fill in the quiet spots in a conversation.

Her self-control was rewarded.

"Yes. Yes. I admit it. I sort-of borrowed a hat from the pizza shop, stuck on a false moustache, and invented an Italian dialect. I knew these were things that Professor Guppy would never notice. They're outside his world view."

"Why, son? You could have asked me for samples. I want my students to become proficient in analyzing materials."

"Listen, Professor, you know I only took the marijuana."

"No, I don't know, Rob. All of those samples landed in a mix on the floor. I have no way of knowing what you took, even if I subtract what we retrieved when we vacuumed the rug."

Mary Beth nodded agreement.

"Listen, that was my marijuana that Austin was keeping for me, hiding it in plain sight. I couldn't just ask for it. I told Mary Beth I'd tell my parents I'm a user…recreational only, and I will keep my promise. I'll tell them, but they didn't know then."

"Do they know now?" Mary Beth asked.

"No, I just told you that. Believe me, I'm going to tell them right after I leave here; that is, if what Professor Guppy said is right, and you'll let me leave."

Mary Beth did not give the immediate permission he expected. "Robby, you didn't only steal." He grimaced. "Yes, it is stealing, even if some articles originally belonged to you. In addition, in a profound addition, I might say, you struck Professor Guppy and knocked him over in order to accomplish what is truly a nefarious scheme."

"No, no I didn't. Just as I reached for the marijuana, the professor started to get up from his chair. I was stretching my arm across the desk to take what I needed at the same time as he started to lean on it. Stuff happened. You know he's unsteady on his feet as well as, well, as well as some other things."

"I beg your pardon, young man. Whatever your name is, I am

not unsteady." With that Professor Guppy took a step down from the booth where he had been sitting and started to do another soft shoe routine.

Am I in the middle of an investigation or a Marx Brothers movie? Mary Beth asked herself.

Humming "Tea for Two," Professor Guppy finished his routine in front of his astounded audience.

"That was my encore," he said a little out of breath. "As far as I'm concerned the show is over. Robby, you've been thoughtless. You've been bad. I expect you to work over-time in the lab this weekend as partial compensation. I'll try to forget all about this."

Of course he will. He won't even remember why Robby is being such a good weekend lab assistant, Mary Beth thought. Out loud she said, "OK, I'll go along with this temporary explanation of the attack on the professor. I'll tell Seth that I'm sure it was kids searching for something in the house, which in fact, it was, and that Professor Guppy will not press charges. Seth won't accept that as a final answer, but he's got so much on his plate right now, maybe he'll accept it for the time being. Having Professor Guppy on your side, Robby, is going to help you immeasurably. If he insists there was no crime at his house, then there was no crime. You owe the professor a huge vote of thanks.

"But, Robby, we know that there was a major crime earlier this month, the murder of Austin Westlake. You and I have to talk."

CHAPTER THIRTY-ONE

"The telephone is a 100-year-old technology… We're getting 80,000 new users each day. And more than half a million people are connected via Skype at any given moment."
—Niklas Zennstrom

Mary Beth Skyped Gabe as soon a she got back to her house after Monday's class. She was glad Tony was out of town again. He was her partner and the person she should call. But what she wanted was to speak with Gabe. He was wise in some ways she was still learning to be.

Although it took seven rings to get through, she tamped down her impatience, knowing he would be at home. One advantage of his being a writer was that she could almost always find him in front of his computer. She laughed when she saw his rumpled tele-vised appearance. He must have been close to literally tearing his hair out.

"Writing problem?" she asked.

"Yes, but it might do me good to take a few minutes off. What's happening with you, dear?"

When Mary Beth told him of her frustrations, that the more she investigated the two crimes, the more confused she got, he said, "Maybe I can help, Mary Beth. I don't know all of the ins and outs of this case the way you do, but remember, I'm a film maker, a story teller. I might be able to weave the various strands together, if you'll tell me what they are. I could finish up with a story arc of beginning, middle, and end that might point to your killer."

"I doubt if it could be that simple, Gabe, though I guess it's worth a try even if telling you everything that happened only helps to clear my mind. I'm sure that Seth is doing a good job. He just isn't moving fast enough for me. I've got this growing compul-sion to find Austin's murderer, but so far, I don't seem to be moving any closer to a solution. I'm solving minor crimes on the side. As to Austin's death, I'm treading water or blood or whatever would make a good metaphor for going nowhere in a murder case."

"OK, Mary Beth, let's handle it this way: first you're going to calm down, then you're going to tell me the whole case, as far as you know it. I don't want every tiny detail. This should take three minutes. Pretend you're pitching me an idea for a film. Go."

"Go?"

"Yes, dear, go! Now."

"I found Austin's dead body. It was horrible. It still is horrible."

"I know that Mary Beth. But now I want the story only. I can fill in the emotions."

"At first we didn't know it was murder. We did know that Austin was worried about foul play either through someone tampering with his bike or by some odd guy named Nat he met on a plane. Both of those paths to solving the crime petered out. They didn't exactly peter-out. They were proven dead wrong. Oops!"

She returned to her narration, "Then by way of Dr. Abby, state labs, and other technical means we learned three important things." She took a moment to mentally examine those facts before she spoke again, "Really, Gabe, those three facts are about all we actually do know even a week later.

"First we learned the time of death, late that Wednesday afternoon, not long before I got there. Then we found out what killed Austin was a poison, belladonna, and finally, that the way of delivering that poison was to mix it with oregano and sprinkle the mixture over an otherwise innocent pizza. So there you are."

"Oh, no" she corrected herself. "There is a fourth fact, sort of a substantiating fact. That's the drawing Austin made on his arm, so clumsy that at first we thought it was a tattoo. Everyone in the various labs concur, he was trying to be as eloquent near death as he had been in life by drawing a picture of the murder weapon, a pizza."

"Good, but you must know more than that."

"Well, yes. Tony and I, I'm going to have to talk about Tony, Gabe."

"I'm good with that. If this were the plot for a really good B movie, he would complete the picture. We would prove that Tony is the villain of the piece and end it in glorious 3-D with you and me as heroine and hero riding off into the sunset together. White horse or your blue convertible?"

"Gabe, Austin was a good friend, not a joke. I'm serious about solving his murder. And Tony and I have had an excellent relationship for a number of years now." She raised her head to Gabe's Skyped picture and caught his eye. "Don't you dare say, 'or so you thought.' Anyway, not one of us is the basis for a joke. Not Austin. Not me. Not Tony either."

Before Gabe had a chance to apologize, Mary Beth remembered what Abby had said about laughter and tears being so close together. Though once-removed from the scene, Gabe's awkward jokes showed that he had been affected, too. No one seemed to know how to talk about death. She removed the scold from her voice.

Gabe was repeating, "Sorry. Sorry, Mary Beth. You are absolutely right."

"As I was saying, Gabe, Tony and I decided that I should casually interview some of my students, the ones who had been showing up in the strangest way at AUSTIN'S art and antiques shop. They were definitely prowling around outside, even prowling around illegally inside the shop. I've used this interview approach for problem solving a couple of crimes before, Gabe, and it's worked."

Gabe regarded her across the Internet with what looked like respectful interest on the blurred television screen. "I don't want to interrupt now, Mary Beth, you're doing a great job of telling your story. Later I'd like to hear more about your career as super sleuth."

"The students in question are a group of four from my American Romantics class—one young man, Robby, and his entourage of three young women. Only it turns out not to be exactly his entourage because he's engaged to one of the women, a naïve young lady from Zambia named Celeste. The other girls are Liz, a congenital liar, and Eleanor known on campus as El from Hell. She's always marching and organizing against something. It took days to arrange all of the meetings with the kids, and what did I learn? Not much. That they were hanging around Austin's shop because he, Austin, was storing Robby's stash of marijuana for him. Robby wanted his pot back and his friends were determined to help him get it."

"So none of them saw anything? Heard anything?"

"They were very focused on weed. What they said they did notice was that, through a series of accidents, Guppy had picked up Robby's marijuana with some other dried leaf materials. What I should mention is that Dr. Guppy's mind occasionally wanders."

"Yes, dear, you've told me that."

"Robby says that he took advantage of that knowledge and what he'd heard about Austin being killed by a pizza to continue with a rather elaborate plan to get his drugs back. I can't imagine why he bothered."

"Kids sometimes like to make things more complicated than they are," Gabe added. "This seems a perfect segue to an admission on my part."

"Now what are you talking about?"

"I feel a little sheepish about this, but I decided that in order to understand the situation better, really, Mary Beth, to understand you better, I should read 'The Purloined Letter.'"

Mary Beth's grin carried over the phone wires.

"I'm going to read you two lines that struck me as pertinent. Poe writes, 'The fact is, we have all been a good deal puzzled because the affair is so simple and yet baffles us altogether.' Isn't that your problem with Austin's death?"

"It's not all that simple though. Robby admits to stealing back his marijuana and in the process assaulting Dr. Guppy. Only he says he was just taking back what was his and accidentally hit Guppy."

"Wow, Mary Beth, assault is more serious than a stolen letter."

"Yes, I'm having second thoughts now. Guppy said he wouldn't bring charges, and I said I wouldn't tell Seth because logically if there are no charges, there is no crime. Right?"

"Wrong. You have to tell the Sheriff. If you don't, legally you would be withholding evidence and morally, no matter how much you like Robby and his family, the facts have to be known. You don't have to exploit your knowledge. You do have to tell Seth Yoder and let him decide what to do and how to use the information."

"Peggy and George will be sick. I can't do that."

"Of course you can. For all you know the information won't have anything directly to do with incriminating Robby, but it might fill in a missing piece of a puzzle Seth is working on."

"I promised Robby."

"Promise me you'll e-mail him as soon as we finish this conversation."

"Yes. You're right. I know it, but..."

"Before we hang up I have one other thing."

"Yes? Do I want to hear more?"

"I love you, Mary Beth."

Mary Beth was happy to hear the words, happier that the screen resolution wasn't clear enough for Gabe to see the emotional effect his declaration had on her. Certain that her blush wasn't visible over the internet, she moved closer to his picture on the screen.

"You sure do know how to change the subject, fast," she murmured.

CHAPTER THIRTY-TWO

"Absence of evidence is not evidence of absence."
    —Dr. Carl Sagan

As soon as she hung up, she phoned the sheriff's office for an appointment with Seth. A bark that she interpreted as "Morse speaking" was the response.

"Inspector Morse?" she asked without thinking, and broke into nervous laughter. "Sorry, I seem to have a cold," she gasped, trying to hide her gaff. "This is Dr. Mary Beth Goldberg calling. I'd like to speak with Sheriff Seth, please." The answer was the buzz of the inter-office communication system, a sound a little less curt than Sylvester's voice.

Seth's greeting was gentler when he picked up the phone. His voice reflected the many hats he wore in his job. Right now he was somewhere between his business and his cow-poke personas, "You say you want to see me, Mary Beth. Mosey on down 'round the middle of the afternoon tomorrow, say three o'clock?"

Mary Beth spent the next morning carefully planning her part of the meeting. She knew no one else took control unless Seth wanted him to. As relaxed as the outer Seth was, the inner Seth was the in charge guy. In this case, she thought he would care about the same things she did, so she could partially relax and let him run the show. She was wrong.

At first he wasn't as interested in her possible contributions as she had thought he would be. When she entered his office, Seth said, "Sit down, Mary Beth, but don't take your boots off. I don't have a lot of time today for civilian conversations."

Mary Beth tamped down her anger. She had come to Seth's office on a worthwhile errand. She said so, "What I have to say is important, Seth. Robby has admitted to being the person who struck, he says accidentally, Professor Guppy." She poured out the whole story.

Seth was then attentive and responded as she had expected he would a few minutes earlier. "You did good in coming here, Mary

Beth. As long as the professor isn't pressing charges, we won't either, but I certainly am going to have a long talk with the young'un." He pushed back his chair as if to get up.

"Give me a few more minutes, please, Sheriff."

"Just call me Seth," he replied, back on automatic.

"A few minutes here, Seth. I want to clear up some other points with you. Austin Westlake's murder has more red herrings than any case I've ever heard about before."

Mary Beth put a stop to Seth's corrective interruption before he could make it.

"You're the detective. I'm not. I know that. But I have been involved in two cases and I read a lot, not just Poe. It's my job. A lot of contemporary detective fiction is based on following the clues in real life cases. What's with us? No matter what clue we have, nothing comes of it. We looked into the accidental bike crash. It truly was accidental. We looked into the tape our paranoid friend left. It turned out to be the result of a practical joke he fell for. We looked into the four students who were hanging out at the scene of the crime. They seem innocent, if odd. We looked into and solved the unrelated marijuana heist from Dr. Guppy. Wherever we look, whatever we question, we find an innocent answer." She took a deep breath.

"As far as I can see, we have only two loose threads we can still follow. We have the pizza shop investigation and the questioning of Simone."

"You're right to a point, Mary Beth, though the department continues to investigate some of the clues you dismiss. Deputy Syl has gone to every pizza shop in Midfield. You'd be surprised at how many there are. In addition to free standing pizza shops, every restaurant that sells pasta, sells pizza, too. After all, this is a college town. And they all make everything 'to go.' Syl has investigated all names available of people who purchased pizzas Wednesday afternoon between one and five p.m. The problem is that no pizza shop keeps complete records of its customers. He also tried descriptions of all possible suspects. As far as Syl can tell, no one sold the mystery pizza to the murderer. As just about everyone connected with this case has said, the pizza could have been bought in a neighboring town or, more likely, months ago frozen at a supermarket.

"We're going back to the beginning. Austin's apartment has

been left alone. It's still a pristine crime scene. Syl is over there now re-fingerprinting what we covered before and including a bigger area. Why don't you re-visit your own ranch, Mary Beth? Maybe you'll find something you overlooked when emotions were running so high. Don't you worry. I'm stickin' to this case like the smell to a skunk's back."

Mary Beth left Seth's office wondering where she should begin reviewing evidence, or, more important, wondering what she hadn't finished first time around. "My conversation with Liz," she admonished herself out loud. *I cut short the conversation to get to Cleveland and Gabe* she remembered. *And I'm glad I did. But I'd better get on the stick now.*

She took out her phone, dialed Liz, and made an appointment to meet in her office within the hour.

As a matter of fact, Liz arrived in Loomis Hall about the same time Mary Beth did and started to talk as they ran up the steps together. "I was going to call you, Professor; I have to talk with you."

Mary Beth pulled the chair from behind her desk so it was at a conversational angle with the guest chair Liz was now sitting in. "I want to talk with you, too, Liz, with the condition that we will have no more lies about your careers or anything else for that matter."

"Oh, I can explain all of that, ma'am, but first I really, really want to tell you something about the day your friend Austin was murdered."

Here we go. Mary Beth leaned forward.

Liz said, "First I'd better tell you that I'm sort of an elected representative. I'm speaking for me, sure. Also for Celeste, Robby, and Eleanor."

"Yes?"

"Well, the day Austin was murdered, I'm not sure how to say this."

"Liz, just blurt it out. We'll put it in order later."

"That's what you always say about writing essays, ma'am."

"Liz, do you want to tell me something that happened on the Wednesday Austin was murdered?"

"Yes, that's just it."

"That's just what?"

"Well, we didn't tell the whole truth then."

Mary Beth bit her bottom lip and forced one hand to clasp the other. Liz had used up all delays. She willed her to talk.

It worked. Liz responded. "Actually Austin asked us to help him." She looked at Mary Beth and saw that her professor thought she meant something more significant than she did. "The four of us. Help him move his furniture."

"Help him move his furniture?"

"Yes, he was worried someone might break in. So we did. Help him move all of that heavy furniture. And that's what we didn't tell Sheriff Seth. We didn't think it was important."

"That's it?"

Liz nodded

Mary Beth recalled Seth's comments about an expanded search for finger prints. *If the group of four was there, he was going to find more than he bargained for. But what would it mean?*

"We'll talk later," she said dismissing Liz while speed dialing Seth with the latest news.

"I don't have time to glory in my finally learning something," she said to him. "You know this is my surveillance night."

"Mary Beth, you're going overboard," was his response.

In fact, she had been thinking of nothing but tonight's surveillance all day. Earlier, she had been impatient to get through class. But the period, which consisted of a discussion of students' term papers, flew by. It was Mary Beth's job as professor to judge the studies as presented, so she had to concentrate. She was happy to find that her students had been thinking, and at least two of the studies would be publishable with a little editing.

Liz's paper on the relationship of the Victorian settings to Poe's work was a blatant appeal to Mary Beth's own line of thought. Her interest in Austin's collection of mid-century modern furniture was public knowledge by now. Liz acknowledged this in the note accompanying her work. Still, the work was solid, well researched, and well expressed. Liz had made some original links. She included internet photos of Victorian furnishings, even a prototype of the all-important filigree card rack of pasteboard where the purloined letter was found. *With work this good, I can hardly hold it against her for playing up to me,* Mary Beth concluded. *Getting on my good side might have been the impetus, but she's gone far beyond that.*

Eleanor's was quite the opposite. She almost angrily proved that today "The Purloined Letter" was too boring to be of any interest to a class and too dated to be applicable to contemporary detective work. She used interviews with Sheriff Seth Yoder and examples from his files to demonstrate that any member of a police force would have found the letter in the first investigation of the room. She had been clever in obtaining Seth's cooperation and used her access to his files and his mind to prove her point.

CHAPTER THIRTY-THREE

"Truth will ouch."
    —Arnold H. Glasow, 20th Century

Now class and the interview with Liz were over, and Mary Beth could start her preparation for the evening's surveillance. It was a little early, but she wanted to be ready. In fact, she couldn't wait. Here was a new experience that was exciting in itself and, because the surveillance was in the Downtown Center, it might, just might, lead her to a clue in the murder of Austin Westlake.

While sharing a pizza a day or two ago, Abby had invited Mary Beth to be a guest at the Final Friday Mensa meeting. The Downtowner Motel, where the meeting was held, wasn't known for its food and Mensa, dependent on home-grown talent, wasn't always known for sterling programs, but Amos was home caring for a sick baby alpaca, and Abby wanted someone to go with her.

As soon as she heard the introduction to the evening's entertainment, Mary Beth was glad she had acquiesced. The speaker was Bonnie Demopoulous, owner and president of the detective agency bearing her name. Her talk was titled, "Not Nancy Drew: A Real-Life Female Detective." Mary Beth had been enthralled.

After the talk, when Bonnie learned that Mary Beth was teaching a course that involved insights into her own favorite detective, Poe's C. Auguste Dupin, Bonnie asked her to come along for a night's surveillance. Mary Beth smiled as she remembered how she leapt at the chance. She waited a few days for a call.

It had come early this morning. After a quick greeting, Bonnie said, "I have an assignment tonight. I'll be in the Midfield Downtown Center area. I can't tell you anything more except that it will be a fixed surveillance. The case I'm working on doesn't warrant movement of the vehicle I'll be using tonight. If you'd like to sit with me and shadow, come along." *Yes!*

Now, preparing for the evening's work, Mary Beth faced the serious problem of what to wear. She had laid out all of her black clothes earlier in the day. From the array on the bed, she chose black gym tights, a black long sleeved t-shirt and black tennis shoes. After surveying herself in the mirror, she topped the outfit off with a black New York Yankees baseball cap someone had given her in her distant past. She carefully went over the white Yankee logo with a black marking pen before putting it on. *Should I put black lines under my eyes?* she wondered. *No, that's football. I'm sure.* She wasn't that sure. She put the black eye-liner in her pocket.

She had been busy all day going to the bathroom as often as she could. She kept up her regime. She also limited liquid intake, abstaining completely after 2 p.m. *What if I ruined Bonnie's stake-out because I needed a bathroom break?*

Finally it was 8 p.m. Mary Beth left the house as secretively as she could and tip-toed down the road to where she had left her car. Her cell phone rang, throwing her into a temporary panic. As she turned it to vibrate, she recognized Tony's number and his style. Not bothering with a greeting, he said, "Mary Beth, I have an appointment tomorrow to tell Seth what I've found out about Simone."

"Who?"

"Simone, Austin's sister. Basically, it's nothing. She's fine." He smiled a smile that Mary Beth could not see. "D'ya want to come along?"

"Yes," she whispered into the phone. This is surveillance night. I'm shadowing Bonnie. I'll talk with you in the morning."

Later she realized how ridiculous she would have looked if anyone had been around to see her tip-toeing and whispering. But everyone was otherwise occupied. When she passed her neighbors' houses, she could see television screens flickering. Thank goodness for the all-American pastime.

As planned, she drove her closed convertible to the Downtowner's parking lot where she left it to join Bonnie, waiting in one of the agency's dark non-descript cars.

Even though a little light was still in the sky, it took Mary Beth a minute or two to find Bonnie's car because it was parked on the side of the lot where it was obscured by large old oak trees whose branches hung over the parking spaces. Bonnie was always the professional.

Before they drove the few blocks to the Downtown Center, Bonnie laid down the law. "Put your cell on vibrate, Mary Beth, and remember, I'm the detective. You're the shadow. I am thoroughly credentialed as a licensed Professional Investigator and Certified Fraud Examiner. You are not, but you can legally shadow a credentialed detective. I take the lead at all times."

Mary Beth nodded agreement. "I figure it's something like driver's ed. Even if you don't have your license yet, you can legally drive when a fully licensed person is also in the car."

Bonnie gave her a look. "That's a stretch, but yes, something like that." She added, "I might even let you eyeball for a while."

"Bonnie, I can't do it, eyeball, if I don't know what it is."

"Sorry," Bonnie answered, "I forget I'm using P.I. slang. It's that on an 8- or 12-hour detail like this, it doesn't make sense for all four eyes to be watching the same site constantly. So every hour or so I'll say to you 'Please take the eyeball for a while.'"

"Got it," Mary Beth answered.

Bonnie started the car for the quick drive to the area where she had started surveillance a few weeks earlier. At that time she had canvassed the selected spots in the area as provided by her client and decided that she had more cover and a better line of sight across the street from the Ye Olde Gaol restaurant than from anyplace else in the Downtown Center, so that's where the two women headed. Mary Beth never did find out what Bonnie's assignment was. She didn't care. She respected this secretiveness as part of Bonnie's professionalism.

She knew her own priorities, too. Here she was, exercising priority number one for the evening, under cover in the Downtown Center, directly opposite Austin's shop. Even two weeks after his murder, she hoped to learn something that would help in solving it. She remembered Tony had written her a note, "for surveillance entertainment," he said when he gave it to her.

She opened it and read, "If you find anything at this late date, you'll be Sheer-luck Holmes." Not exactly the encouragement she needed.

An hour passed. Nothing happened. Bonnie was taking meticulous notes in preparation for her client's report. Through the car's legal tinted windows, Mary Beth watched the empty streets. Out of boredom, she started to ask questions, "Do you ever take photographs or videos?"

"Not at night," Bonnie smiled, "but during the day. Sure."

"Would they ever be interesting for a non-client to see?"

"I dunno. I have some stills with me that I made from an afternoon video I took in Midfield two weeks ago Wednesday. I was just about in the same location."

Mary Beth started to thumb through the dozen or so still frames Bonnie had handed to her. She immediately recognized Robby and his posse of three entering Austin's shop. "These are invaluable, Bonnie. The sheriff will definitely want to see the video they were taken from. They even have identifying geographic and time markers on them."

"Can you FedEx me the video tomorrow? On second thought, could you FedEx it to me care of the sheriff's office? I have the address right here."

Mary Beth looked up from the pictures she was holding just in time to see a lone couple headed toward Ye Olde Gaol's parking lot. *Was that?* She wouldn't permit herself to finish the thought. *No, it couldn't be.*

She didn't have to self-censor.

Sirens cut off thoughts. Lights flashed in the women's eyes. Motorcycles surrounded them. The seat belt kept Mary Beth from hitting her head as her body took over with a startle response. Threatening leather-jacketed male bodies were visible through the window. Mary Beth and Bonnie rolled down their windows so they could be seen as the innocents they actually were.

With gun and taser at the ready, Sylvester Morse and a rent-a-cop had them surrounded. "Get out. Hands above your heads."

"Mary Beth? That can't be you!" In the midst of shouting orders Sylvester stopped. To be certain what he was seeing, he lifted his mirrored sunglasses (*At night?* Mary Beth wondered).

"Sir," Bonnie said authoritatively. "I have notified the sheriff's office that I am a private detective and would be in this neighborhood conducting surveillance tonight with my assistant." She smiled at Mary Beth.

"I still have to see your I.D.," Syl blustered, arms akimbo, flashing his Elvis belt buckle.

Mary Beth remembered that she was the Indian; Bonnie was the chief, and for once said nothing.

After Sylvester sniffed around Bonnie's credentials for a few minutes and could think of nothing more to do but to release the women, Bonnie turned to Mary Beth with a shrug. "Well, our cover is blown for tonight. I'll take you back to your car. I hope you got something out of this."

"It was a great experience, Bonnie, even before I saw the photographs. They're the tops; they're the Coliseum. Never mind, I'm beginning to sound like one of my students."

"You're beginning to sound as if you're dehydrated. It's a side effect that bothers women P.I.s more than men. Think about it."

CHAPTER THIRTY-FOUR

"All some folks want is their fair share and yours."
—Arnold H. Glasow, 20th Century

The next morning when Mary Beth took the photographs to Seth she got a more dramatic reaction than expected. Coming from Seth, it was an absolutely explosive response, albeit silently explosive. After one look at the photographs, Seth put on his cowboy hat. He pushed back his chair and stood up. Then he said, "Let's go. No moseying this time."

Mary Beth followed him out the door to the street where his buddies were, as usual, sitting on the bench he had donated.

"Hey, Irwin. Hey, Daryl."

"Howdy, Sheriff," replied Irwin for the group.

"Just call me Seth," was the expected follow-up.

"Warm enough fer ya'?" Daryl asked.

Again cutting short the ritual, Seth took the conversational reins in hand. "Fellas, do you remember a month ago Wednesday, the day Austin was killed?"

"Shor do. We don't have many murders in Midfield. It were right over there."

"You told me you saw three or four of the students go into the shop."

"Thet lassy right there, too."

"Yes, yes the teacher. Her name is Mary Beth and she's a friend of mine, too."

"Howdy," said Mary Beth, mentally kicking herself for falling into the good ole boy vocabulary game.

"Howdy, ma'am," was the reply accompanied by a joint half-rise from the bench. With Joe standing solid in the center and Daryl and Irwin each leaning in toward him, the men managed the nearly smooth rise and lowering back to their seats required by mid-Western politeness.

Seth reined in the conversation again. "You told me you saw three or four students go into the shop. I was wondering if you could remember which number it was."

"You were jist 'wonderin'?" Irwin repeated. "Thet horse won't run once around the barn, Seth."

"Nope, thet 'wonderin' dog ain't gonna bark, Seth," said Daryl expanding on the theme.

Seth smiled at his friends, who could be as wily as he was.

"Well," Irwin said, smiling back and looking to his pals for approval, which he got. "We talked 'bout it some more. There was four of them, three gals and one feller."

Mary Beth and Seth looked at each other. The surveillance photographs that Bonnie had given to Mary Beth clearly showed three people leaving Austin's building. Just as clearly, the photos showed that the three people were Celeste, Liz, and Eleanor. Where was Robby? The three young women would know.

"Those three girls are coming in for questioning as material witnesses. Right now. Do you have their phone numbers in your cell, Mary Beth?"

Mary Beth did.

The sheriff made his calls on the spot, moving a few feet away from the "old-timers club" for privacy. Seth was the kind of person who expected people to pick up their phones when he called, and the three new witnesses did just that. He also was the kind of person who did not accept excuses. His home spun persona gave way to a tough professionalism.

"I can't come right now because I have a class."

"You can come right now because I tell you to."

"Can you make it tomorrow? I'm doing some research in the library?"

"I can't make it tomorrow and neither can you. The appointment is today."

"I'm awfully busy right now—Giggle. Giggle."

"You'll be awfully busy in a holding cell if you don't get yourself down to my office right now."

When he finished the calls, Seth turned to Mary Beth with something more than a request, "I want you to sit in on the questioning. The college wants to control its own disciplinary actions. It doesn't want the police stepping on its administrative toes. But this isn't shop-lifting. It's a murder. I'm going ahead with the investigation, no matter what any dean or president thinks. And I want you to be present, so I have an official faculty member of Midfield Campus College as witness."

As they started to walk back upstairs to Seth's office, Mary Beth nodded her agreement. She had expected as much. *I've done plenty of work toward solving this murder, if it's actually going to be solved in Seth's office. He should recognize my role.*

"I'm not sure you heard everything I said, Mary Beth. I'm going to repeat, 'I want you to *sit in* on the questioning.' I do *not* want you to take part in it," Seth said, oblivious to Mary Beth's wounded ego. He added, "You can take notes, if you want, and talk with me tomorrow."

What? Who gave you the photographs, Seth? Who followed up on that odd prankster, Nat? Who carefully, subtly, and with distinction interviewed all of the students involved?"

She remembered that people are supposed to manage their anger. As she was asking herself, *Do I want to be in this investigation or out?* The FedEx truck drove up. *That answers it.*

CHAPTER THIRTY-FIVE

"It's possible to solve a mystery and still not know all the answers."
—Terence Faherty, *Prove the Nameless*

Mary Beth signed for the package Bonnie had addressed to her. Seth followed her as she ran up the steps to his office and computer. She was surprised to see Tony seated and waiting. *He must have come in through the alley door, the one usually reserved for delivery of corpses*, she figured. She gave an involuntary shiver as she realized that it was about a month to the day that Austin's body had been delivered through that same door.

Seth acted as if he had expected Tony. *In fact, he had*, Mary Beth said to herself as she remembered Tony's phone call from the previous evening about his appointment with Seth. Greetings were exchanged and folding chairs pulled into the small area that was Seth's private space.

It had taken Mary Beth a few minutes to realize that Seth was no longer playing the role of her down-home, cow-poke buddy. He radiated authority as he turned the meeting temporarily over to Tony.

"Before you start, Tony, I want to make sure everything is above board. As I'm sure you've figured out, you and Mary Beth are the amateurs and those in this office are the professionals. We have questioned and followed Simone, too. You might as well man up to the fact that we probably know everything you know."

Tony's face reddened.

What's that about? Mary Beth wondered.

Seth had his horse blinders on. He had a murder and a possible robbery to solve. He continued, "I will want to hear any information you may have picked up about Simone or Austin. She might have some sibling insight."

"Simone doesn't know anything about the crime, Sheriff Seth."

"Just call me…"

"Gotcha, Seth. The only thing Simmy said that might apply toward motive is that Austin liked to think he was more important than he was."

Mary Beth exclaimed, "That would explain the imagined death threats on the tape he left for me. If you think about it, why would anyone want to kill him?"

"Well, Mary Beth, someone wanted to and did, kill him, that is."

"What about the lettering on his signs with just his name in capitals?

You have to admit that's a little self-important and odd," she added.

"But aren't we all," Tony muttered.

Seth looked at each of them in turn. "We have an almost positive identification of the unsub. What we're going to find out right now, is it unknown subject singular or plural. So, stop the quibbling. Whatever's going on here, it's not helping to solve a serious crime."

Mary Beth and Tony tried to erase the various guilty looks that flitted across their faces.

Seth loaded the disc into computer. The recording started with static and double exposures in the places where Bonnie had obliterated scenes that were part of her P.I. files.

Then on the small screen, Seth, Tony, and Mary Beth saw clearly the three young women as they were leaving Austin's shop.

Just as they realized what they were seeing, they heard those same three students plus Robby thumping up the steps and arriving at Seth's open office door in time to see themselves on the surveillance film.

"What's going on?" El asked.

"That's what we'd like to know," Seth said.

"I want to talk with you one at a time, but I want you all in the waiting room until it is your turn. It won't take long.

"Liz, you stay in this office for now."

As her friends filed out, Liz nervously twisted her long blond hair, pulling it in front of her face as she did so.

She's trying to hide, Mary Beth thought. *Is she concealing something worse than her lies?*

Seth had become avuncular. "Liz, he said I've been watching you for a few weeks now. Something is going on. Whether it has anything to do with the murder of Austin or the robbery of Professor Guppy, I don't know. Maybe you have a basic need to lie;

maybe you have been trying to ingratiate yourself with your professors, flattering them by fantasizing jobs in their fields. Whatever your need is, it has not shown up in any of your school reports until this semester. And it has shown up in an odd way. Reportedly you have told various people on campus that you want to be a circus roustabout, a parachute jumper, a lepidopterist, a forensic dermatoglypher, the author of an e-epistolary novel, a scientist in an avian cognition and language lab, and goodness knows what else. Is this correct?"

Liz blushed. "Almost," she said. "Actually I did work for a short time with a circus last summer, though I wasn't exactly a roustabout. I sold programs." She peered at Seth from behind her hair, took an audibly deep breath, and dragged out an answer to his question, "Yeeess, it's correct."

She added quickly, "But I'm not supposed to talk about it."

Seth looked at her. "Elizabeth, this is a murder investigation. It supersedes any 'not supposed to talk about it' in your life. You'll tell us right now what is going on."

"I'm innocent. The whole thing is innocent. I'm part of a social-science investigation from the University of Pennsylvania. They got volunteers from a couple of different colleges. We all had to use a little deception to gather material for a study. I thought you guys would catch on when my mentor, Dr. Felten, wrote an article about it for the *Wall Street Journal*. But maybe you just read academic stuff."

"Some of the dust is settling around the corral, but I still don't know what's going on here."

"I know you guys don't like this, don't like all the different careers I made up. Well, that's what the researchers found out. They got enough evidence to show academics don't like to be duped."

"Why that's completely unethical," Mary Beth responded. "If I did a study on you and other students without telling you about it, I'd be up before the faculty senate for unprofessional, if not illegal, behavior. You can't run a study on people without their permission."

"They do in social-psychology," Liz pointed out. "In fact, that's really what I'm going to major in. And," she added, almost defiantly, "I'm writing my senior thesis on my experiences in using deceptive information at McCollege."

"Sounds like it belongs in the manure pile to me," Seth replied, "but that's for your college to decide. I'll need some names and contact numbers for this Dr. Felten and your other research buddies. I expect you to stay around until I contact them. Then I reckon you're free to tell any more whoppers you want."

Liz left, temporarily triumphant.

Eleanor had designated herself as the next interviewee.

Mary Beth noted that El looked more and more like an illustration for one of Poe's short stories. Now her hair, parted in the middle, hung straight and raven-dark over her shoulders.

Seth continued to conduct the interviews, based in part on information received from Mary Beth. At first, he suspected that El's proposed transfer to the U. of Chicago was, in fact, her plan for a legalized get-away. To prove his point, Seth led her through a series of questions ascertaining the dates of visit to the university, inquiry letters, application, and acceptance. He had to admit that her story was unexpectedly legitimate. "From what you're telling me, Eleanor, and what you told Professor Goldberg, all of the required paper work was taken care of long before Austin's murder, not as a result of it. I'll need proof."

El was indignant. "You might not like what I say. No one around here does. You people aren't used to hearing the truth when it's not covered up with mid-Western politeness. Don't worry I'll scan the required forms to you as soon as I get out of here and back to my dorm."

Unimpressed with attitude, Seth concluded the interview, "El, I don't want you to mess up your new stable before you get there, but if those papers aren't on my desk within the hour, I'll call Chicago and get copies from them."

CHAPTER THIRTY-SIX

"'The riddle, so far, was now unriddled.'"
—Edgar Allan Poe, *The Murders in the Rue Morgue*

As Eleanor left the room, signaling thumbs-up to her friends, Robby called out from the waiting room, "Can I be next? I don't want to put Celeste through any more of this. She doesn't have to be upset." He walked toward Seth's door where he could see Seth nod agreement.

"That's kind of you, Robby."

"She doesn't need this. I've made enough trouble for her," he said as he tried to juggle himself, his bulky knapsack, and books into a condensed package that would fit in the office. "Really, Austin made the trouble."

"What do you mean by that?"

"He kept bragging about how he had some of Poe's letters written to the Allan family, the people who took Poe in. Every time I said my dad was in trouble with his department, Austin would say, 'Well if he had some of the letters I have, his reputation would be made.' Then he'd offer to sell them to me for money he knows I couldn't possibly have. Or is this 'the imp of the perverse' talking? Am I giving myself a motive?"

"It would come out sooner or later, Robby. We have photographs of four people entering Austin's on Wednesday, the 23rd, the day of the murder, and only the three female students leaving the shop. These photos are evidence. They mean you could have stayed, gone upstairs to share your poisoned pizza with Austin, found the papers and left, thinking you had committed the perfect crime. More, we have Austin's eloquent tattoo."

Robby laughed. "You're almost right. With one minor exception. There were no letters. I had most of the day to search for them. Later, when I checked sources, it dawned on me that Austin made it all up to make himself seem important. He played me. He got what he deserved. No missing letters of Poe's exist at all. I should have done my research ahead of time."

They heard a wail from the waiting room, an eerie soundtrack to Robbie's explanation.

"The girls knew didn't they?" Mary Beth asked.

"They must have," Robby replied. "I've been on a journey of self-destruction for a long time. Poe would have understood."

"I don't, Robby. Aren't you at all sorry about this?"

"As my dear friend and, I guess former fiancée, Celeste, would say, 'Yes, regrets, I've had a few, but then again too few to mention.'"

His own imp of the perverse dominated as he continued with, "Yes, if I'd only put the poison in Rice Krispie marshmallow cookies instead of a pizza, you'd never have suspected me. You'd still be looking, looking for a cereal killer."

"Stop it! Stop it, Robby." Mary Beth became stern while the other horrified adults absorbed the tragic scene.

Seth started to read to Robby, "You have the right to remain silent. Anything you say can and will be used against you in a court of law. You have the right to speak to an attorney…"

Mary Beth and Tony faded out of Seth's office, quietly shooing the three girls ahead of them out of the waiting room.

EPILOGUE

"Who breaks the thread, the one who pulls, the one who holds on?"
  —James Richardson

As Mary Beth and Tony walked in shocked silence to nowhere in particular, Mary Beth kept reminding herself that she had to talk with Tony about their relationship. She couldn't figure out how to go about it. *I can't just say to him, "Guess what's new, Tony."*

What she said instead was, "The situation is so awful. Robby will end up in prison even though Abby's arranging for psychiatric help for him. He really doesn't understand the depravity involved in what he did. Instead of helping his family, he's devastated them. Leavin' alone what he did to Austin."

Without waiting to hear if Tony was aboard, she continued on her own track. "Speaking of Austin, I decided to offer the course he was helping me with for next semester."

This brought a puzzled, "What?" from Tony who was on his own track, too, and only half paying attention to Mary Beth.

"You know. I listed the course as 'Mid-Century Modern in Literature and Furniture.'"

"Yes?"

"Nobody, that is, no one at all, signed up."

"I wonder why," Tony murmured in a sotto voice.

Then Tony, still following his own thoughts, made the peremptory conversational strike: "Mary Best, and you are, can we talk about something else except Robby and Austin?" He didn't stop for a reply.

"This is kind of related to his crime. Well, kind of, I never would have met, well..." He stammered again. "Look, Mary Beth, I have a meaningful Ph.D. from M.I.T. I've worked for a few years with my hands repairing bicycles. I confront material reality every day. Some people think because the work is dirty, it's also stupid. They're wrong. I know from cause and effect in ways that few of my peers do. And I have an information age resume. I was willing to put much of that aside because of you. But we're going no-place. No place. We're great at solving crimes together." He smiled. "We're great in bed together. But I want to get on with my life and I mean, beyond being Bob's partner. Good, but not good enough."

"Tony, are you trying to tell me that you… you've found someone else?"

"Yes, I am. I have. I feel terrible about this. There is someone else, Mary Best. Honest, I wasn't looking. I wasn't interested in anyone else."

Mary Beth's pride allowed her to think it possible.

"At least, I thought I wasn't looking. I was trying to help you, so when I went to Akron on business, I looked up Austin's sister Simmy, excuse me, Simone. I'm sure you've heard of the theory of unintended consequences.

How many bike shows did you think Akron had? Your mind must have been on something else, too, or you would have noticed how much I was out of town and how busy I was when I was here in Midfield."

Mary Beth's mind shot back to a few nights earlier. When she had been on surveillance, she knew she had seen a familiar looking couple leaving Ye Olde Gaol restaurant. She couldn't admit it to herself then. She did now.

Tony's head was bent down in guilt. His whole body was bent over as he said, "I'm sorry, so sorry. I never meant it to end like this. I never meant it to end."

He felt his color change as he added what he thought he had to, "I'm going to work for Simmy's father. Manny Westlake owns a bicycle factory. I'll be running it." He finally stopped his nervous rant of extraordinary excuses and abject apologies to look at Mary Beth for her reaction.

He was amazed to see a huge smile infuse her face with radiant joy.

OTHER ANAPHORA LITERARY PRESS TITLES

Evidence and Judgment
By Lynn Clarke

East of Los Angeles
By John Brantingham

Death Is Not the Worst Thing
By T. Anders Carson

The Seventh Messenger
By Carol Costa

Rain, Rain, Go Away...
By Mary Ann Hutchison

Truths of the Heart
By G. L. Rockey

Interviews with BFF Winners
By Anna Faktorovich, Ph.D.

Compartments
By Carol Smallwood

CPSIA information can be obtained at www.ICGtesting.com
Printed in the USA
BVOW021435190412

288039BV00001B/13/P